Sin Lieth at the Door

Arbor Vale Mystery Series

Sin Lieth at the Door

Arbor Vale Mystery Series

Book V

Eunice Loecher

This book is dedicated
to my favorite creative writing place,
Little Creek Coffee Company in Arbor Vitae, Wisconsin.
Thank you for your encouragement and support.

CONTENTS

CHAPTER ONE

Zita Stillman waited impatiently for her company to leave. Her celebration with friends and family had taken an unexpected turn with the sudden arrival of her son, James and her daughter-in-law, Heather. Their presence left Zita in a state of anxious confusion. They appeared unannounced, pulling a U-Haul trailer. Not a good sign.

Zita's widowed niece, Kimmy Camden, gave welcoming hugs to her cousin and his wife. Kimmy introduced them to her seven-month-old daughter, Kyla then, working her way around the table, she pointed to Police Officer Roger Brooks and his young son. The elderly Gem sisters came next. And finally, Daniel Edward, an old friend of Zita's.

Zita's dearest friend and cousin, Zinnia Blossom Winwood, didn't wait for an introduction; she jumped up to embrace both Jim and Heather. "Honey, I can't remember the last time I saw you. And I've never met this beautiful wife of yours," she gushed.

Jim grinned. "Zinnia, you haven't changed a bit. From what I hear, you and Mom are still getting into trouble all the time."

Zinnia bobbed her head. "We try. We sure do try. That's why we're having this celebration."

Daniel went to get two extra chairs for the table as Zinnia told the story of all that had happened in recent weeks with the Arbor Vale Hotel project. Zita busied herself preparing warm plates of their special Thanksgiving dinner in April.

Her daughter-in-law remained silent and sullen during the entire hubbub.

Once everyone resumed their seats at the table, Zinnia turned to Heather.

"Sweetie, you're awfully quiet. Are you feeling okay?"

"We've had a long day on the road and we're both tired." Jim jumped in before his wife answered.

Daniel raised his eyebrows inquiringly. He apparently understood that Jim's unexpected visit meant something serious had occurred.

After half an hour of pleasant chatter around the table, the Gem sisters gave discreet yawns. Zinnia offered to drive them home. Roger and his son left next, followed by Daniel.

When Daniel walked out the door, he whispered to Zita, "Call me if I can help."

"Thank you." She pointed to the U-Haul. "Something has happened. Heather hates coming to northern Wisconsin. She considers Arbor Vale the end of the civilized world." Zita's stomach churned. She dreaded returning to the kitchen and facing her son. He had apparently brought a severe problem to her door tonight.

By the time Zita returned to the kitchen, Jim and Heather were finishing up their pumpkin pie and coffee and Kimmy had started cleaning up.

Zita joined her niece at the sink, motioning toward the bedrooms. "Our little girl is getting sleepy. Isn't this Kyla's bedtime? I'll finish up here."

Kimmy gathered her daughter from the highchair. "Thanks, Auntie. Goodnight, Jim, Heather. We'll catch up in the morning."

Left alone with her son and daughter-in-law, Zita poured another cup of coffee and joined them at the table. After stirring in some cream, she waited for Jim to speak. The silence draped heavily on Zita. Her anxiety grew more intense with each passing second.

Heather threw her napkin on the table. "Well, go ahead and tell her, she's your mother." Tears gathered in her eyes.

Zita cringed at Heather's angry words. The situation continued to escalate. Things between her son and daughter-in-law were worse than she had imagined. Heather's tears caused Zita to long to comfort her, but any word or touch would probably be rebuffed.

Jim took his wife's hand. "Honey, I promise to straighten everything out. This is only temporary."

Heather pulled her hand free and dabbed at her eyes with a tissue.

Apprehension exploded in Zita's chest. Heart pounding, she waited for Jim to explain. For the first time she noticed the gray hairs at his temple. Worry lines creased his forehead. "Are you ill, Son? Please, tell me what's wrong."

"Mom, we've lost everything. What's left of our lives is in that U-Haul in your driveway."

"I don't understand. You were both doing so well," Zita said, searching for a possible explanation.

"What they say is true; you're only a few paychecks away from living in your car," Jim said. "What else could we do? We had nowhere else to go."

This unexpected news stunned Zita. She sought for words of comfort and encouragement. She touched her son's arm. "You're both welcome. I wish you had contacted me. I might have been able to help. There's the recent inheritance from Aunt Elsie."

"Mom, the way things were, you would have been throwing your money away. First the bookstore where Heather worked went out of business. Then the hotel I managed filed for bankruptcy. Things continued downhill. Our investments and retirement accounts tanked. Neither of us has been able to find another job. And soon we were behind on the rent. That brings us to Arbor Vale."

Their problems poured over Zita in a torrent. She had longed for her son to live closer, but never under these dire conditions. And certainly never forcing her daughter-in-law to come to a place she disliked so much. They would need to stay in the apartment downstairs short term. The apartment Kimmy used as a bed-and-breakfast business. Once the hotel renovations were complete, Jim and Heather could move in there. With her head pounding, Zita concentrated on possible solutions to these overwhelming problems.

A month later

Zita stood at the patio door, gazing out over Arrowhead Lake. She loved living on the lake, experiencing the changing seasons. The trees surrounding the lake stood stark and leafless. Some had formed buds which wouldn't open for several weeks. The only color came from the tall pines. Their varying shades of green needles formed a canopy reaching toward the sky.

Today was the opening weekend of fishing season in her small northern Wisconsin town. Zita hadn't found any solution to all the difficulties that plagued her son and daughter-in-law. Each day she prayed for ways to lift the burden of hopelessness that blanketed her home. Heather made it clear she resented any offers of help from Zita. And her disdain for Arbor Vale became more and more obvious.

They had endured four weeks of brooding silence from Heather. She left every morning, returning after supper. Zita had no idea where she spent her days. Jim spent his time job hunting locally and sending out resumes. He also pitched in at the Arbor Vale Hotel, working with Daniel to complete the restoration.

Zita hoped to open her newly inherited business any day now. She had heard through the usual gossip channels that Zinnia planned some extravagant open house as a surprise to celebrate the new venture. Zita had been the recipient of one of Zinnia's parties in the past. A stressful event filled with over-the-top elegance. Zinnia tended to be over-the-top in every part of her life.

Putting her coffee cup down on the table, Zita noticed the alarming activity taking place in front of her home on Arrowhead Lake. Something was wrong. Gravely wrong.

Kimmy joined her aunt at the door. Wearing jeans and a denim shirt, Kimmy balanced Kyla on her hip. "What's going on out there? Why would they bring in the police dive team? Did something happen to one of the fishermen?"

Zita removed a pair of binoculars from a cabinet drawer. She observed the men in the water. "They're diving over the fish crib."

Kimmy shaded her eyes from the sun's glare bouncing off the water. "Fish crib?"

Zita handed her niece the binoculars. "Are you able to figure out what's going on?" She refilled her cup from the coffeepot on the counter. "Fourteen, no, more like fifteen years ago already, your uncle Lorman and Jim built a fish crib on the ice. When the ice went out, the crib sank."

Kimmy handed the binoculars back to her aunt. "I've never heard of a fish crib. What does it look like?"

"We had a nasty ice storm in November that year," Zita explained. "We lost five or six huge old oak trees. Lorman and Jim hauled twelve-foot lengths out onto the ice. They constructed a square box four logs high and chained them all together. Later, they filled the crib with brush and extra concrete bricks. When the ice went out, the fish crib sank."

"So do the mommy fish keep their babies there?" Kimmy teased.

Zita grinned. "No. But the crib does provide a safe habitat for the smaller fish. The whoppers hang around outside hoping for a nice meal. And that makes for a good place to fish."

"Is that Roger docking a boat at our pier?" Kimmy asked, shading her eyes again.

Apparently most of the police were on duty this busy weekend. Roger wore a new suit instead of his police uniform. Uneasiness shuddered through Zita. Whatever had happened on the lake might involve them. She opened the patio door, waiting for Roger to climb the steps up from the lake.

"Something's wrong." Kimmy said.

The fact that Roger's mouth was spread into a grim line only increased Zita's anxiety. Something terrible had apparently arrived at her door. This time, she hoped the news didn't involve another murder.

Unsmiling, Roger stepped inside. "Kimmy. Zita," he greeted them.

Zita's fingers curled into her palms. She didn't want to hear what Roger had to say. Swallowing hard, she managed to croak out a few words. "Please, sit down." She motioned toward the kitchen table. "Would you like a cup of coffee?" She continued to stall. "Nice suit. I heard you've been promoted to detective. Congratulations."

Pulling out a chair, Roger barely acknowledged Zita's words. "Thanks. No coffee." He sat down heavily, removing his ever-present notebook and pen.

Zita slid onto a chair across from him. She interlaced her fingers tightly in her lap.

Kimmy paled, staring at Roger. "What's going on? What happened out on the lake?" Her voice trembled.

That's why I came to talk with Zita," Roger responded. His voice held an ominous quality.

Zita cleared her throat. Bad news needed to be handled like a sticky bandage—rip fast and deal with it.

Kimmy pulled out a chair and sat down, transferring Kyla to her lap. "Whatever involves Auntie Zita, involves me. Now what's going on?"

Having Kimmy as an ally encouraged Zita. Together they'd handle whatever news Roger brought.

Roger surveyed the kitchen. "Is Jim here?"

"No, he's working with Daniel at the hotel." Did this involve her son? She became more uncomfortable with Roger's presence by the second. "Does this have something to do with Jim?" Uncertainty made her voice tremble.

Roger's gaze remained fixed on Zita. "Tell me about the fish crib."

"Auntie Zita told me Uncle Lorman and Jim built it fifteen years ago," Kimmy blurted out, sounding confused.

Zita's fear grew. Without knowing what had happened, she didn't want to say anything further to Roger. "Before I answer any more of your questions, do I need a lawyer?"

"There are questions that need to be answered." Roger said.

"Roger, what's wrong?" Kimmy demanded. "You act like someone has been murdered."

When Roger didn't respond to Kimmy's accusation, Zita started to shake. "Something bad has happened. What did you find in the crib?" She feared his answer. Why else would Roger come to her home asking questions? *Please, not another murder victim.*

Roger tapped his pen on the tabletop. Zita recognized his nervous habit. Something he did when upset and agitated.

"The fish crib," Roger said. "The records registered with the Department of Natural Resources show that your husband built the crib. Did you help him with the construction?"

"No, he built it right after the ice storm we had that November. Jim graduated from college midterm that year. While job hunting, he stayed here and helped his dad build the fish crib." Her jaw tightened. *I'm babbling.*

Roger made a notation in his notebook. "Two fishermen were over the crib this morning. One got his line snagged. He managed to pull up the snag, and also a human skull. The divers discovered more remains chained inside the crib."

7

Kimmy gasped. "Roger, no. That's horrible."

Zita forced herself to take a breath. Was Roger accusing her husband and son of murdering someone and burying them in the fish crib? The victim had remained buried in her lake for the past fifteen years. "Who?"

Roger didn't blink. "Do you have any idea?"

Kimmy exploded. "Roger, are you accusing my uncle and cousin of murdering someone?"

He stared Kimmy down. "I'm not accusing anyone. These questions have to be asked, either by me or someone else. Zita would want to cooperate with the investigation."

Zita wrapped her arms tightly across her chest. "Kimmy, please calm down. Roger's right. These questions have to be asked. That is our fish crib, built by my husband and son. But we did not murder anyone and hide the body in the lake. Are they able to identify whether the victim is male or female?"

"The thicker, heavier skull and pronounced jaw line belongs to a man. They'll examine the remains for DNA. We need to find out who went missing around the time your husband built the crib."

Zita shut her eyes and shuddered. A horrible memory surfaced. "Clive," she mumbled. Even his name brought a sour taste into her mouth. He had been vindictive and evil. Took pleasure in harassing his victims.

"Who is Clive?" Roger and Kimmy asked simultaneously.

"Clive Chatwyn." Zita said. "He left town fifteen years ago. There were problems."

"What kind of problems?" Roger persisted.

Zita sighed, weary of the questions and the memories. "Mostly rumors. Clive worked for the Department of Natural Resources. You'll get more information by talking with them. And Clive's wife and daughter live in the area."

Once again Roger focused on Zita. "Someone mentioned that your son, Jim, left town permanently then too?"

"Roger, stop. Do Auntie Zita and Jim need a lawyer?"

The memories chilled Zita. "I don't have anything more to say on the subject."

Roger's jaw clenched. "Jim's at the hotel with Daniel?"

"They're working there together every day," Zita replied.

He stood, putting his notebook into his pocket. "Thank you. You've given me a place to start." He turned and left by the patio door.

The color drained from Kimmy's face. "Auntie, what's going on?"

Zita ignored Kimmy's question and raced to the phone and dialed her son. "Jim, listen. Roger left here and he's on his way to talk with you. A fisherman pulled up human remains this morning in the lake. The fish crib. Divers have been down. Apparently someone went through the ice inside the crib. He asked if anyone who had gone missing around that time. I mentioned Clive Chatwyn to him. I'm sorry. I spoke without considering the consequences. Call me when he leaves." Zita hung up the phone, steadying herself by gripping the edge of the counter. The ticking of the clock remained the only sound in the kitchen.

For the next half hour, Zita paced, waiting for the phone to ring. Kimmy had badgered her with questions. Unanswerable questions. Zita couldn't understand why Clive's name had popped out. She wanted to snatch her words back. In the future, she'd be more careful when answering Roger.

Kimmy demanded to know about Clive. Zita wasn't able to tell her very much. He had made many enemies in their small community, including her family. And especially her son. Clive hadn't been the reason Jim left Arbor Vale. But Zita had been relieved when her son had been offered a good job in Chicago. That's when Clive disappeared.

"I'm sorry, Kimmy. I don't want to speculate until they identify the body," Zita said. "These old stories don't need to be brought up and discussed. I said too much to Roger already. Why won't Jim call?"

A shudder of dread raised goose bumps on Zita's arms. A dead body in her fish crib—think of the rumors and innuendo this gruesome discovery would provoke! Jim should tell Heather about Clive Chatwyn and his daughter. If those old rumors resurfaced, they might cause further damage to their relationship. Would friends and neighbors believe that her family had killed Clive Chatwyn? Unfortunately, there would be more than a few who'd assume they'd done the town a favor.

When Zita heard a car door slam in her driveway, she raced to the door. Her son had come home. How much he resembled his father—the same muscular build, black curly hair, and hazel eyes. He reminded her of Lorman in other ways too: his calm assessment of situations, never overreacting. She hoped those traits would fortify Jim in this touchy situation.

Jim started reassuring her as he came up the sidewalk. "Mom, don't worry. I talked with Roger. I'm sure he doesn't believe I killed Clive."

"Good. But you need to tell Heather about Jodie Chatwyn. Your wife shouldn't have to deal with rumors. If that is Clive's body, gossip will be running wild."

Jim looked Zita straight in the eye. "We are not responsible for the body they found. And there is nothing for Heather to understand. Nothing."

Zita was surprised at how relaxed and upbeat Jim appeared. He exuded trust and confidence. Working at the hotel with Daniel this month had made a positive impact on him. She wished the same could be said for Heather. Some of her anxiety melted away. But not all. This murder had been laid at her door.

Jim led the way into the kitchen, "Besides, there are a few other things I need to discuss with you."

Uneasiness spurted back into the pit of Zita's stomach. "Let's sit down." She pointed toward the kitchen set. Sitting down across from him, she waited. Her hands were clasped tightly in her lap.

"Mom, this month has shown me how much I've missed Arbor Vale. Everything. The lakes, the woods, the friendly people. And I've enjoyed working with Daniel. He's a lot like Dad."

Zita swallowed past a lump forming in her throat. Would her son decide to stay here? But suppose Heather spoiled her idyllic dream. Heather, with her weeks of brooding silence, tears and sullenness.

Jim's eyes sparkled when he announced, "Mom, I'd like to manage the hotel. I have experience in that area. Would you consider hiring me as your new manager?"

Whatever Zita had expected, Jim's request hadn't been on her list. Oh, she'd wanted to suggest it, ever since the Gem sisters had moved out of the hotel. She needed a manager, and Jim would be the perfect solution. Now that he and Daniel had finished remodeling the manager's apartment on the main floor of the hotel, Jim and Heather could move there.

The possibility of having her son nearby was blessing. But there was only one huge question in Zita's mind. Her daughter-in-law had made her feelings about Arbor Vale perfectly clear. She decided to confront the elephant in the room head on.

"How will Heather react? Have you talked to your wife?"

"Daniel and I have been discussing the possibility for the past few days," Jim said. "I wanted your opinion before talking with Heather. I'm sure she'll be excited."

Zita cringed. She saw only a huge disappointment for her poor son. Heather would not be happy with this development. Didn't he notice the way his wife had been acting all these weeks? She hated everything involving Arbor Vale. *Including* me. Was love that blind? Did she dare warn him? Or not interfere?

"You'd make a wonderful manager for the hotel, and it would take a huge burden off my shoulders. I've been putting off advertising the position."

Jim shoved his chair back and stood up. He walked around

the table to give his mother a hug. "Mom, this is a new beginning for Heather and me."

A new beginning. Zita wanted to believe her son. But…

"Mom, you need to come and see the apartment." Jim sounded like a teenager instead of a forty-year-old man. "I'm planning to spring the surprise on Heather tonight when she comes home."

"I'll tell Kimmy where I'm going and get my coat." Zita couldn't catch even a smidgen of Jim's excitement. All she could think of was Heather's anger and frustration with being stuck in Arbor Vale.

CHAPTER TWO

Zita sat beside Jim in Daniel's pickup truck. Since Heather used their car, dropping Jim off at the hotel in the morning, Daniel generously let her son use his truck during the day if he needed it.

Around them, tourist traffic swirled. Mentally making to-do lists, Zita's thoughts were just as chaotic. Their bed-and-breakfast would be filled most days. Customers would be flowing through her woodworking business. The hotel needed to be managed. Soon Daniel's campers would arrive. She hoped her community would accept those groups of at-risk city kids. Especially after all the protests and negative petitions that had circulated in recent months.

Zita's greatest apprehension hinged on Heather's reaction to Jim's plans. She didn't even know where her daughter-in-law spent her days. A question she needed to ask...delicately.

"Mom, you're quiet. Is something wrong?"

"I'm wondering about Heather. How has she adjusted to life in Arbor Vale? I rarely get a glimpse of her."

"You think Heather is avoiding you. But she isn't. She's been working part-time at the bookstore and volunteering the rest of her free time at the library."

This was news to Zita. Heather rarely spoke to her. And Jim had never been a great communicator.

Jim's words sounded as though they were merely an excuse for his wife's behavior. He hadn't answered her question. "But is Heather going to agree to stay?"

Jim's boyish excitement faded. His eyebrows drew together, his hands tightening on the steering wheel. He gave a dismissive shrug without answering.

Zita's spirits plunged. She had hoped her son would remain in the area. But she didn't control the choices of others.

When they reached the hotel, Daniel met them at the door. He greeted Zita with a pleased grin. "Did Jim tell you his news? Things would work out great if he manages this property."

Still worrying what Heather's reaction might be, Zita replied as honestly as possible. "He certainly would be the perfect replacement for the Gem sisters."

Daniel's brow furrowed. "Do you have concerns about Heather?"

Zita didn't want to discuss her son's marriage now. Not in front of Jim. After working with her son this past month, Daniel had to be aware that there were problems.

Jim walked toward the apartment at the back of the lobby. "You're in for a surprise, Mom."

They entered the apartment, and Zita stared at the transformation, her mouth open in amazement. "Oh, Jim, you and Daniel worked a miracle in here." The walls of the kitchen were painted a soft green. There were new appliances and countertops. All of Jim and Heather's things had been moved in and arranged.

As Zita started toward the bedrooms, the hotel door banged shut. Through the open apartment door, she could see Heather stomping across the lobby. Anger like vapor rose and surrounded her daughter-in-law. Jim ushered them out of the apartment.

Zita shoved her hands into her pockets. If Heather saw the apartment before Jim had an opportunity to explain, there would be an explosion. She winced, wishing to be somewhere else.

Anywhere but here.

"I hate this town," Heather thundered. "I've lived in the city all my life and nothing like this ever happened to me." She scrutinized Jim, Daniel, and then Zita. Her face melted into a deeper scowl. "What's going on?"

Jim stepped forward, draping an arm around Heather's waist. "Nothing. I wanted to show Mom some of the new improvements." He attempted to turn his wife back toward the lobby. "What happened? Why are you here?"

"I'll tell you what happened. Someone stole my purse." Heather's cheeks blossomed into a shade of rose. "I expected to be safer in a small town. Bunch of thieves. And they're afraid of bringing in a bunch of city kids. Give me a break."

"Honey, calm down," Jim said. "Who stole your purse?" He rested a hand on her arm.

Heather shrugged off his hand. "How should I know? My purse is gone."

Zita started edging toward the door. She didn't need to be part of this.

The hotel door opened again and Myrtle Percy hobbled in with her cane. She adjusted her glasses on the bridge of her nose, peering into the dimly lit lobby. "Zita, Zita Stillman, is that you?"

Zita crossed the lobby. "Yes Myrtle, I'm here."

"Your niece told me you had come to the hotel." She lifted her hand, waving a black leather purse. "Does this belong to one of your relatives? Somebody named Heather Stillman."

"Where did you get my purse?" Heather demanded. She lunged toward Myrtle, grabbing the bag. She inspected the contents, counting her money.

Zita gasped at her daughter-in-law's rudeness. "Myrtle Percy is one of Arbor Vale's sweetest, kindest, and most honest women." She bit down on her lip to keep from saying things she might regret. But Myrtle handled things for her.

Amusement flickered in Myrtle's gray eyes. Her lips twitched. "Ms. Stillman, you left your purse on the roof of your car. When you pulled out of the library parking lot, it fell into the road."

Heather flushed with embarrassment.

"I couldn't catch up to you," Myrtle continued. "You sure drive fast-like in the city. Hurry. Hurry. Hurry. I followed you to the bookstore. But you were already leaving, and I lost you in traffic. That's when I located your name. I assumed you must be one of Zita's relatives. But you don't act like one of Zita's family."

Zita pressed her lips together to prevent the grin from bursting out. *You go, Myrtle.*

Myrtle glowered silently at Heather for a few seconds. "Young woman, I saw you inspect your wallet. I'm not a thief. I spent a good part of my afternoon tracking you down. At the very least, as common courtesy, I would expect a thank-you. That's how Arbor Vale folks act. But then again, you're from the city."

Myrtle turned toward the door, giving Zita a wink. Zita grinned in response.

Heather had the decency to mutter an apology. "Mrs. Percy, I'm sorry for my rudeness. Thank you for going to all this trouble to return my purse. I was very upset when I thought my purse had been stolen. But that isn't an excuse. I hope you can forgive me."

Zita gazed at Heather in utter disbelief. An apology. Her daughter-in-law sounded sincere. She experienced a glimmer of hope. All that defiance and anger might be a pretense concealing...what?

As Myrtle continued out the door, she gave a grunt of satisfaction. "Apology accepted."

Heather turned toward the apartment and the open door. She jerked back around. "Why is my kitchen table in that apartment?"

Zita's stomach muscles clenched. She couldn't handle another Heather meltdown today. Side stepping quickly, she decided to escape now. Daniel hurried out the door right behind her. The last words she heard was Jim saying, "Honey, I have a surprise for you."

❋〽 〽❋

Daniel joined Zita on the sidewalk outside the hotel. "Your daughter-in-law is a bit of an enigma," he commented diplomatically. "Jim has hinted at an estrangement with her parents. However, I doubt even he's aware of the whole story."

Zita found Daniel's observation disconcerting. Heather an enigma? Maybe. But Zita knew nothing of problems in Heather's past. The first time she met her daughter-in-law had been at the lawyer's office during the civil wedding ceremony. The service lasted ten minutes and none of Heather's family members were present. There had never been an explanation for their absence.

"Daniel, I don't understand. I've rarely spoken to Heather since their marriage ten years ago. I've never been invited to their condo in Chicago. And whenever Jim called, our conversations were brief. He led me to believe they had this busy wonderful life in the city. I just assumed they didn't have time for a widowed, dowdy mother. What did he tell you?"

"I'm sorry, Zita. If Jim hasn't mentioned anything to you, then I must treat our conversations as confidential." He lowered his voice. "Here comes Zinnia. Too late to dodge the inevitable."

Zita didn't have the patience to handle Zinnia just now. Her focus was on Heather. Were there serious problems in her past? Problems so serious that Jim wouldn't share them with her?

Zinnia charged up, babbling as usual. "I'm glad I caught you both. What did Myrtle want? Was Heather at the hotel? She rarely goes inside. Usually honks for Jim in the evening. I want your permission and approval for a party I'm planning for the grand opening of the hotel. Surprise! Were you going to change the name to something jazzier? 'The Arbor Vale Hotel' doesn't have any charisma. For promotion you ought to do a name-the-hotel contest. Offer a prize of one free night at the hotel."

Zita waited. She knew it was useless to interrupt Zinnia once she got going.

Zinnia gave an exaggerated shiver. "To chilly to stand around gabbing. Come on down to the beauty shop. We can zap out our plans in no time."

Zita grabbed onto Daniel's arm. She didn't intend to tackle this daunting task without moral support. He followed along, grinning at her consternation and Zinnia's endless chattering.

Finding the beauty shop nearly empty was a blessing. Zita generally had qualms discussing anything with Zinnia. At her beauty shop—gossip central—Zinnia and her girls usually spread Zita's business all over town within seconds.

Zinnia led them to her office in the back of the salon. Zita chuckled at Daniel's dazed expression. She should have warned him. The interior flowed on a sea of pink from the vinyl chairs to the sinks and hair dryers. The entire staff of beauticians wore pink smocks. The combination of the glaring pink decor and irritating smells from the hair products caused Zita's eyes to water. She noticed Daniel blinking his eyes.

Zinnia plopped down on a chair behind her desk, waving them toward two molded pink plastic chairs. Her desk held a jumble of papers and empty coffee cups. She managed to pull a clipboard from beneath the hodgepodge. "Ah, here are my notes. I decided a Saturday or Sunday afternoon might be best. Nothing fancy. Finger food, desserts, coffee, and punch."

Zita started to relax. Her eyes had stopped burning from the permanent wave solution and hairspray in the air. This sounded doable. Not the usual Zinnia disastrous extravaganzas, like the exploding chocolate fondue fountains, or the potbelly pigs escaping from a petting zoo. Zita's favorite event had been the six-foot-tall inflatable rabbit. Zinnia filled the large balloon with too much air. When the rabbit popped, the cake and punch exploded into the mayor's lap.

Zinnia's bifocals were resting on the end of her nose. She peered through them, struggling to decipher her notes. "Oh, yes. I remember. Daniel, this would give you a chance to plug your camp. You'd explain how the children will be helped by this opportunity, etc."

Daniel leaned forward. "That's an excellent idea, Zinnia. I might be able to answer some of the questions the town residents brought up previously. Particularly those raised by Beatrice and Floyd Torkel."

The Torkels. Zita winced at the mention of their name. *Agitators.* That couple thrived on creating strife in Arbor Vale.

"Now that the remodeling at the hotel is complete and if Heather agrees, they can move in and manage things. Time for the camp to begin." Daniel said. Boyish excitement filled his voice. "I've been in contact with a pastor from Madison who has a group of four young boys lined up to come. I'll check with Jim and make sure Heather has agreed and they're ready."

Ready? Zita wanted Daniel's camp to succeed. They had planned for this day. But once again, everything threatened to overwhelm her. Everything in her life continued to move too quickly. Reservations for the bed-and-breakfast were picking up. She scarcely kept up with the orders for her woodcraft pieces. And she didn't have the slightest idea how to run a hotel. All of this plus now, they found a body in her fish crib.

"Oh, this is all so exciting," Zinnia twittered. "I didn't realize Jim and Heather planned to manage the hotel. You must be thrilled to have them staying in Arbor Vale."

Zita cringed. Would Heather agree to Jim's plan to manage the hotel, even temporarily?

Zinnia continued her outburst without pausing for a breath. "And next weekend is the Penny Parade too. I'm doing a float again this year."

They were interrupted by one of the beauticians. She eyed Zita with a mixture of curiosity and cool appraisal. "Could I speak to you privately for a moment?" she asked Zinnia.

Zinnia gave her employee a quizzical look. "I'll be right back," she said, standing and following the employee out of the room.

When Zinnia returned she sat down and stared across the desk at Zita. Her eyes narrowed, and her smile flipped into a pout.

19

"So girlfriend, is there something you may have forgotten to mention? Like a body found in your lake?"

Zita bit her lip. *The body.* The memory chilled her. Forced to find out news of another murder victim through ordinary gossip channels would make Zinnia furious.

Daniel stiffened. "Body? What's happened? And please, Zita, tell me this doesn't involve you in another murder."

Zita didn't want to talk about the victim. "Someone fishing over the fish crib snagged a human skull."

Zinnia gave a soft gasp. "Gross."

Obviously stunned by the news, Daniel asked, "Who?"

"A dive team came out and found the rest of the body still chained in the crib. Roger said the victim, a male, had gone down with the fish crib fifteen years ago."

Zinnia groaned. "Is that the one Lorman and Jim built? Oh, Zita, do they imagine your family murdered someone and hid the body?"

Zinnia's words expressed Zita's every fear. People would readily spread such evil gossip. Leaning forward, she gripped the edge of the desk to stop her hands from shaking. "I hope not. Roger already spoke with me and then Jim. First they need to find out if anyone locally went missing during that time."

Zinnia waved her hands in the air. "I'll bet they found Clive Chatwyn. That's when that egotistical jerk vanished. The town should have had a celebration."

A muscle quivered in Daniel's jaw. "Clive Chatwyn? I remember him as a real bully."

Both Zinnia and Daniel had the same opinion of Clive Chatwyn and his disappearance. Zita's memories of Clive were vivid. Even after all these years, they brought a bitter taste into her mouth. He had remained mean and aggressive from childhood to adult. He had been the poster boy for sexual harassment. Women avoided him. He had been bigger and stronger than the other boys, using his strength to pound those around him into submission.

The salon door banged shut. Heather stormed in, heading straight toward the office. This day kept getting worse. Zita's private nickname for her daughter-in-law had become "Hurricane Heather." And if Heather's expression indicated her mood, they were in for a tempestuous squall.

Heather stopped in front of Zita, towering over her. "How dare you go behind my back and convince *my* husband to even consider staying in this dinky backwater of a town."

Daniel stood, jamming his hands into his pockets. "Young woman, lower your voice. And I'd appreciate a more respectful tone. Zita knew nothing of Jim's plans until this morning. If you want to blame someone, start with me. Your husband suggested that managing and living at the hotel would be a positive, though temporary solution, to your current difficulties. Obviously, by your attitude, you must have a better plan."

Zita noted the color flooding Heather's cheeks. Dear Daniel, he had come to her defense again. Tears gathered in Heather's eyes. She wiped at them with the back of her hand. "I'm sorry Zita." Turning to leave she mumbled, "For better or worse. This is the worse."

Heather's words jolted Zita, filling her with apprehensiveness for her son and his marriage.

Zinnia popped out with one of her quotes. "According to Doug Larson, 'More marriages might survive if the partners understood that sometimes the better comes *after* the worse.'"

Physical and mental exhaustion engulfed Zita. Weary of all the drama, she wanted to get in her car and start driving anywhere away from here.

Daniel stood over her, concern etched into his face. "Zita, is there anything I can do?"

Zita gazed up into his azure-blue eyes. "Daniel, it's just one thing after another."

He sat down next to her. "Don't give up. Jim loves Heather and wants his marriage to survive this trial." His deep, mellow voice echoed in the small office.

The stress of the day had taken a toll on Zita. Tears filled her eyes. "Thank you, Daniel. You've spent time with Jim this past month and understand him and his situation better than I do. I'll continue to hope." She turned toward Zinnia. Her lifelong best friend hadn't said a word since sharing the quotation. Her countenance had become a study in sadness and regret.

"Zita, forgive me," Zinnia begged. "Your life has exploded."

Exploded? Zita tested the word. Yes, her life had exploded. Pieces of her had been ripped off and spewed in all directions. Why had the quiet life she lived only a year ago vanished?

Zinnia stood, walked to Zita, and enveloped her in a bone-crushing hug. Tears trickled down Zinnia's cheeks. "And here I go, blithering on and on about an open house, the Penny Parade, and the dead body in your fishing crib."

"You're forgiven. I'd rather celebrate the wonderful possibilities the newly remodeled hotel might bring to Arbor Vale. And the Penny Parade is an exciting event." Zita remembered the first Penny Parade held in 1953. She had been in kindergarten at the time but marched with her entire school class, waving small American flags. "I'm letting the police sort out the victim found in my lake. That has nothing to do with me or my family." Determination resounded in her voice.

"Let Roger, the newly appointed county detective, do his job." A flash of amusement flickered in Daniel's eyes. "I'd forgotten the celebration for Dr. Kate and the million penny collection. The following year she was a guest on that television show, *This is Your Life.* The pennies poured in after that and built the hospital."

"I loved Dr. Kate's nickname, Angel on Snowshoes," Zinnia said. "She helped deliver me. That's one of the reasons I participate in the parade, to honor her memory."

"It was the math teacher at the grade school who started his students collecting the pennies," Zita added. "He wanted them to have a concept of a million of something. And they donated all those pennies to build our hospital."

"Is 'The World's Largest Penny' still standing on the corner by the grade school?" Daniel asked.

Zinnia walked back to her desk and sat down. "The school has been torn down, but they saved the penny. The monument is still on the corner. Except now an assisted living facility has been built on that site, The Penny Place."

"Perfect name. I'm glad our little piece of local history is preserved," Daniel said.

Zita switched to the present. "Is there anything that needs to be done before the hotel opens?"

Daniel counted things off on his fingers. "The industrial washers and dryers have been installed in the basement. All the bedding and towels have been delivered. Jim is ready to manage the property and handle all the bookkeeping and reservations. We have two local students lined up do the laundry and cleaning. They aren't available for the first two weeks, so until then, Kimmy has volunteered to pitch in. Jim had hoped Heather would help. But I doubt that will happen."

"Kimmy offered to help? She didn't mention anything to me. How can she add that to her many other responsibilities?" Besides caring for Kyla and operating the bed-and-breakfast, Kimmy had started taking a few on-line classes to qualify for a teaching position in Wisconsin.

One of the beauticians entered the office. "Zinnia, your last appointment is here."

Zinnia shoved back her chair and stood up. "Duty calls. Will you ride on my float this year, Zita?"

Visions of previous parades danced in Zita's memory. During her high school years, she marched with the band, playing her flute. Another year she rode on her church's float. In recent years she'd ridden on Zinnia's float and had found it harder to be as inconspicuous as she'd been before. There were the colorful wigs Zinnia insisted she wear. Then the piles of makeup. And of course those bright pink smocks. In spite of all this, there was only one possible answer. "I have so much fun throwing candy to the children along the parade route. I wouldn't miss riding on your float for the world."

"Good. Daniel?" Zinnia asked.

"Sounds like fun, but I'll be busy at the hotel," Daniel said.

As she hurried into the main salon, Zinnia waved her fingers in their direction. "Au revoir. I'll handle everything."

Zita started to giggle.

"What's so funny?" Daniel asked.

Zita managed, barely, to bring her amusement under control. "Sorry, Daniel. When Zinnia asked you to ride on her float, I pictured you in one of her wigs and a smock."

Daniel's eyes sparkled with humor. "And that's exactly why I refused so quickly. I pictured the same thing. Why are *you* willing to expose yourself to a Zinnia makeover?"

"Glutton for punishment," Zita quipped. "Zinnia means well with her exuberant transformations. I pretend to be someone else. But really, I enjoy interacting with the happy excited kids." She folded her hands, interlacing her fingers. "Daniel, I'm worried Kimmy's doing too much. When my shop is closed, I'll help with the cleaning in the evening."

"The two students will be available on weekends," Daniel said. "Then full-time once school ends for the summer. Jim and I plan to help Kimmy. Her life is busy, especially with Kyla. The hotel should be fairly quiet until Memorial Day weekend. If Jim gets overbooked, I'll call you. Thanks for offering." His usual smile slid into a frown. "I still pray that Heather's heart will soften and give Arbor Vale and Jim a chance."

Zita clasped her hands tightly together. She didn't plan to stop praying for her daughter-in-law. But her misgivings surrounding Heather continued to grow. No matter what Zita did, she couldn't break through the wall that encircled Heather; each day that wall grew thicker and harder to penetrate.

"Your daughter-in-law is a very vulnerable and frightened young woman," Daniel commented. "She expresses that fear with a sharp tongue. Your patience with her is remarkable."

The compliment caused heat to rise in Zita's cheeks. "This

past month hasn't been easy." *That's an understatement.*

"Not easy for you or Jim. But your support and attitude has helped Jim. They're struggling right now. But those struggles started long before their financial meltdown. God has brought them here for a second chance. Love them and allow God to work."

Brushing away tears, Zita agreed. "I can do that, Daniel. Yes, I can love them."

Doctor Kate, Angel on Snowshoes

1885-Kate Pelham born in Wellington, Kansas.

1913-Attends medical school at the University of Buffalo, New York.

1917-Graduates and begins internship in New York City followed by residency in Detroit, Michigan.

1921-Dr. Kate marries William Newcomb.

1922-Moves to northern Wisconsin.

1931-Dr. Kate receives Wisconsin medical license.

1949-Fund started to build a Lakeland area hospital.

1953-May 30 Million Penny Parade held in Woodruff, Wisconsin. 1.7 million pennies collected.

1954-On March 17, Dr. Kate appears on *This is Your Life*. On April 6 Dr. Kate delivers the first baby in the new hospital. "The World's Largest Penny" is dedicated on July 21.

1956-Dr. Kate dies during hip surgery.

The Doctor Kate Museum is located at 923 Second Avenue, Woodruff, Wisconsin. The museum opened in 1988 as part of Woodruff's centennial celebration.

CHAPTER THREE

Thursday morning as Zita climbed the hotel stairs with an armload of sheets and towels, Zinnia bounded into the lobby. "Girlfriend, we have to talk. I'm moving the open house to tomorrow afternoon."

Zita listened in bewilderment, becoming exasperated with all the modifications to the original simple plan. Zinnia's latest to-do list was becoming increasingly difficult to manage. Why had she ever agreed to this party? There wouldn't be time to make all these changes.

Zinnia's eyes narrowed, giving her friend a sharp glare. "Are you even listening?"

"Attempting to keep up with all your changes."

"Today is Thursday. This is short notice to pull things together." Zinnia tapped her pencil on the reception desk in the lobby of the hotel. "But the open house has to take place tomorrow afternoon."

"Why?" Zita asked, unable to control her thoughts. They scampered from one problem to the next. She walked back down the staircase.

"The first group of campers will arrive tomorrow night."

Zinnia scribbled something on her clipboard. "The Penny Parade is on Saturday afternoon. You're riding on my float. We can't be in two places at once."

Zita draped the linens she had been carrying on the desk. She had expected Daniel and Jim to handle the open house. But she had to agree with Zinnia. Daniel would be preparing for his first group of young boys and their chaperones. Jim couldn't handle everything alone. Heather certainly hadn't made any effort to help. "You're right."

"Of course I'm right. I've given this mega consideration," Zinnia huffed. "Still planning to keep things simple. Hired the same caterer I used at your house last January."

Unease skittered through Zita. "Caterer? We planned to keep this simple."

A mischievous gleam came into Zinnia's eyes. "Simple? What's simpler than having someone else do all the work? Especially the cleanup, girlfriend."

"Is everything ordered? How much will all these preparations cost?" Zita bit her lip. Everything in her life continued to gyrate out of control.

"All you have to do is show up. This is my treat." Zinnia grinned, licking her lips. "The buffet will be amazing."

"I can't let you." Zita touched her friend's hand. "This is too much."

"I love to throw parties." Zinnia raised her chin, patting at her fluffy blond hair. "And besides, I want everyone to remember this wingding. It might set the tone for the whole summer."

That's what Zita feared. Zinnia's parties created a gossipy stir for weeks afterward. But her mouth started to water for all the scrumptious food the caterer would prepare. His petit fours melted on your tongue.

"I don't have to offer you a penny for your thoughts. I do believe you're starting to drool." Zinnia laughed. "Come early. The food will go fast. We're starting at two o'clock tomorrow afternoon."

"You caught me dreaming of petit fours." Zita chuckled.

Gathering up her papers, Zinnia grinned again. "I can taste Carl's pecan pie melting in my mouth." She paused. "Until tomorrow. I guarantee this party will launch the hotel."

"Thank you for doing this," Zita called after her friend. She knew if the hotel became a successful draw to tourists, their business might revitalize the main street. She picked up the linens to go upstairs again. Daniel and Jim would be back soon with some last minute supplies for the first group of boys coming to the weekend retreat.

Zita's emotions switched from anticipation to dread. Would people only come out of curiosity over the body found in the fish crib? Beatrice and Floyd Torkel might come and make a scene. She paused halfway up the staircase, her jaw tightening. What if the protesters came? That unpleasant couple thrived on creating trouble. Daniel's dream of these short retreats for at-risk city kids would succeed. If only the Torkels would stay away.

The hotel door opened and Heather walked in. She glared at Zita. "Is Jim here?" Her voice held a bitter edge.

"No. He's out with Daniel," Zita said. "But I expect them back in a few minutes." She kept her tone gentle. "How has your day been going?"

Heather ignored Zita's question. She continued walking to the apartment at the back of the lobby.

Rebuffed, Zita continued up the stairs and into one of the bedrooms. She spread out the fitted sheet, tucking under the corners. Her thoughts remained on her son and daughter-in-law. The previous Monday, Jim and Heather had moved into the apartment in the hotel. When they left her home, Zita experienced relief mixed with guilt. The entire month they lived with her had been tense. Heather avoided any contact with her or Kimmy. If they were forced to be in the same room, Heather ignored them and pouted. Everything Zita said or did only strained the relationship further.

Zita heard footsteps coming up the staircase. Daniel and Jim must have returned.

At the same time, she heard angry raised voices coming from downstairs. Her son and his wife were fighting again. Jagged painful sorrow weighed upon her. She sat down on the nearest chair. Closing her eyes, she covered her ears with the palms of her hands to shut out the harsh words.

When a hand touched her shoulder, Zita jumped. She looked up at Daniel, reading sadness in his eyes.

"Are you okay?" he asked softly.

The fighting had ended. A door slammed. "I feel helpless."

"I understand." Daniel said. "But your son is a lot like you. He finishes what he starts. And he won't give up on their marriage."

His words brought a soothing balm to Zita's raw nerves. "You've spent more time with Jim this past month than I have. More time than I have in the past ten years. You're the best mentor for him. Thank you."

"I've enjoyed our time together," Daniel replied. "He's a good man. There are no guarantees, but I believe they will be able to work through these problems."

She wanted to believe Daniel. But as he said, there were no guarantees. Zinnia's proposed party came to mind. Daniel hadn't heard the change in plans. "Zinnia stopped in a few minutes ago."

Taking a step backward, Daniel grinned. "Oh no. Do I want to hear this?"

"Probably not. She's moved the open house up to tomorrow afternoon."

Daniel folded his arms across his chest. "Tomorrow? How can we be ready?"

Zita raised her hands. "Everything will be fine. This will work better. The party won't interfere with the Penny Parade. Your boys won't be here yet. Zinnia and I can help. Best of all, Zinnia hired a caterer to handle everything."

Daniel relaxed, sliding his hands into his pockets. "Wow! That does sound good. Zinnia planned this?"

Zita chuckled. "Yes. She said she put mega-thought into this."

"Mega?" Daniel grinned. "She should do that more often. I'll tell Jim the new plan."

"What new plan?" Jim asked, walking into the room.

Zita noticed how tired her son looked. More than tired, worn out and depressed. Was this due to all the changes and work at the hotel? Or maybe this involved Heather and their marriage?

Daniel filled Jim in on the plans for the next afternoon. Jim's face held a mixture of frustration and determination.

"Is there anything I can do, son?" Daniel asked.

"My marriage is hanging by a thread and right now that thread is unraveling. And Heather probably wishes she had married Jonathan Stanbury."

"Who is he?" Zita asked. She had never heard Jonathan Stanbury's name mentioned.

Jim's jaw tightened. Frustration oozed from him. "The guy Heather's parents wanted her to marry. Family friend and Wall Street broker. When she chose me, they disowned her. That's why we married in a lawyer's office. No big wedding. They even refused to come." He twisted the wedding band on his finger. "The only reason Heather hasn't left already is because she can't face her parents. There's an, 'I told you so' waiting for her there."

Some of Zita's irritation directed toward Heather evaporated. The things Jim revealed explained a lot. But why did Heather continue to act like the spoiled princess? Zita understood feelings of abandonment by one's parents. Her mother had rejected her, leaving her to be raised by an elderly couple. A mother who had refused to acknowledge her existence. The past still hurt. Feelings she had tried to bury bobbed to the surface.

"Zita?" Daniel's voice pulled her back to the present.

She blinked. "Sorry. I was, what's the saying, 'woolgathering'? Daydreaming and lost in my own little world." She focused her attention on Jim. "Heather doesn't like me, and I haven't found a way to change her opinion."

Jim started to protest.

Zita cleared her throat. "Honey, Heather doesn't hide her

animosity toward me. Right now that doesn't matter. Is there anything I can do that won't make matters worse?"

"Sorry, Mom. There isn't anything I've done that makes a difference." As he turned to leave the room, his shoulders drooped. "I have paperwork to finish. I'll see you tomorrow."

With a pang of regret, Zita acknowledged that both Jim and Heather were adults. And Heather would resent any interference.

Voices echoed up from the lobby. Zita recognized Jim's voice. She strained to hear who the other person might be.

"Sounds like Roger is here," Daniel commented. He turned and left the room.

Zita followed. By the time she reached the top of the stairs, Daniel had already joined the two men in the lobby.

"They've identified the body. I'm going to the police station with Roger to answer a few more questions," Jim said.

Leaning into the wall, Zita gripped the railing, her hands trembling. Roger must be here because the victim is... "Who?" She barely managed to choke out the one word.

"Clive Chatwyn." Roger said, resting one hand on the reception desk.

Covering her mouth with her hand, Zita fought for self-control. Roger scrutinized her reaction.

Zita lifted her chin, determined to survive yet another chaotic event dropped into her life. "Have you spoken to Clive's wife and daughter yet?"

A muscle quivered in Roger's jaw. "Never an easy job to inform next-of-kin. Even after all these years." He picked up his cap from the desk. "I won't keep Jim long. I may need to talk with you again, Zita."

Licking her lips nervously, Zita's hand gripped the railing tighter. She wondered how Clive's wife, Suzanne and daughter, Jodie, were handling the news. Should she contact them? Offer sympathy?

"Later, Mom," Jim said, following Roger out the door.

After a restless, sleepless night, Zita arrived at the hotel Friday afternoon to help with the open house. She wanted to keep any vivid images of the investigation buried deep inside. How many years had she fished over that crib? The image of pulling up a human skull terrified her. At times like this, she longed for the comfort and protection of her husband.

She wished Kimmy had been able to come today. But her niece had remained at home with Kyla. During the baby's nap, Kimmy had been busy cleaning the downstairs apartment. Heather hadn't made an effort to tidy up when they moved out. New bed-and-breakfast guests were expected after supper.

"Too much. Too much," Zita mumbled. When she reached the door, Zinnia zoomed out, nearly knocking her down.

"Whoops. Sorry, girlfriend." Zinnia gave a twittery giggle. She gripped Zita's arm to steady her. "Carl the caterer has certainly worked his magic on the hotel lobby. Wait until you catch your first glimpse. I'm absolutely agog with the transformation. Have to buzz down to the beauty shop. Need to do a quick change."

Quick change? What was Zinnia planning? Clinging to the door handle, Zita paused to calm her jittery, overstrung nerves. What would she find in her hotel lobby? "Now or never," she mumbled, turning the handle and stepping inside.

The lobby had been transformed into a festive party atmosphere, celebrating not only their grand opening but the Penny Parade. Oversized, sparkling copper-colored penny garland hung from the ceiling and decorated the walls. Crisp, white linen cloths covered the tables. The center pieces were a mixture of copper candle holders and penny-shaped vases filled with bright yellow tulips.

Carl approached Zita. "Mrs. Stillman," he said, "is everything to your satisfaction?"

"This is amazing, Carl. Overwhelmingly beautiful."

"Good. Good." Carl preened. "After the Penny Parade tomorrow, I have a big gala event at the town offices. You did give too short of a notice for this party." His brow wrinkled. "I've decided to use the same decorations and meal plan prepared for the town. And *voila*, behold, we have a celebration." Leaning in, he lowered his voice to a whisper. "Besides, sharing the decorations will save you and the town a bundle."

Chuckling to herself, Zita watched as Carl darted away to correct one of his servers. She closed her eyes to savor the delicious aromas permeating the lobby. Carl certainly created memorable events.

From behind, someone touched her arm. Jerking around, she came face-to-face with Zinnia. Her friend had returned, wearing a copper-colored fluffy wig. Zinnia apparently had returned to the beauty shop for this unfortunate, unattractive choice. She apparently sought to blend with the décor, striving to be a penny.

"Well, is this mind-blowing or what?" Zinnia demanded.

A loaded question if ever Zita had heard one. *Definitely mind-blowing.* "You have captured the essence of the penny."

"Oh, good." Zinnia patted at her hair. "I might be inspired to wear this in the parade tomorrow. Of course, I'll have to dress my costume up a bit." She paused, her eyes narrowing as she studied Zita. "I have another wig that will fit you perfectly. We'll be the smash of the parade."

More like a train wreck, Zita thought. Fortunately before she could reply, Heather entered the room from the apartment at the rear of the lobby. Once again, Zita found herself staring. Heather had her brown hair curled and caught with a sparkling clip behind one ear. She wore a slinky black cocktail dress. The single shoulder strap, shaped like a lightning bolt, ran down the front of the dress. Stunning, but overdressed for Arbor Vale.

"Whoa," Zinnia gasped. "Is that Heather? She's smiling. She never smiles. That dress is stunning. She's stunning. What gives?"

Zita cringed, glancing down at her comfortable jeans and

long-sleeved Penny Parade T-shirt.

"That's quite a turnaround," Daniel commented as he joined them. "I wonder what's motivating Heather."

"She looks amazing and happy. Whatever her motive, this is an improvement." Zita took in Daniel's attire: jeans and a matching long-sleeved T-shirt promoting the Penny Parade. Pointing first at his shirt and then hers, she chuckled.

They responded in unison, "Great minds think alike."

Daniel's rich deep laughter rolled across the lobby.

Zita noticed Jim approach Heather. He kissed his wife's cheek. She didn't respond, turning away. A twinge of disappointment threaded through Zita. Apparently, Heather hadn't dressed to please her husband. Instead, had she planned to draw a sharp contrast between Arbor Vale and uptown and classy?

Striding up to Zita, Carl glanced at the wall clock. "Time to unlock the door and welcome your guests." He gestured toward the tables laden with food and flickering candles.

With a springy bounce in her step, Zinnia unlocked the door. Immediately, people poured into the lobby. Zita found the sudden crowd overpowering. They scrambled everywhere like an army of ants on the march. Hungry ants.

Acting as hostess, Heather floated around the room, smiling and greeting their guests. Feeling unnecessary, Zita wondered why she had bothered to come.

Across the room, Daniel motioned for her to join him. Zita pressed her way through the throng. The din of conversation drowned out any coherent thought.

Daniel raised his voice above the crowd. "Could you handle the tour of the upstairs rooms? I'm fielding questions concerning the kids coming to the area tonight."

Zita offered him a thumbs-up as a reply. Now she had a useful purpose in being here. Several people followed her up the staircase. The door to the attic remained padlocked. Momentary panic slithered through her. The memory of what had been discovered in the attic, her attic, still held disturbing power over her.

As they inspected the rooms, she enjoyed the pleased surprise of the guests. Several of the older members of the community remembered the hotel during the glory days of the late 1920s and early '30s. None of the gentleman confessed to having been a customer, however.

During the tours, Zita caught a few guests trying the doorknob to the attic, unsuccessfully. *Morbid curiosity seekers.* Thankfully, the secret the attic contained had been permanently buried. The antique furniture and clothing had all been moved to the Gem sisters' new home. Swept clean, the attic no longer hid anything from the past.

An hour into the open house, Zita heard shrill shouting from the lobby. Rushing down the staircase, she found Beatrice and Floyd Torkel having a confrontation with Ruby Gem. Anger had flushed Ruby's face scarlet. Hands on her hips, she stood nose to nose with Beatrice. Timid Pearl Gem cowered behind her sister.

Zita move through the crowd to reach the enraged women. Daniel stepped between them first.

"Ruby, please, what's wrong?" Daniel's voice remained calm.

"No one talks about my mama and papa the way this woman did," Ruby spouted. "She had better take back those words and apologize."

With a smirk, Beatrice took a step back. "I won't apologize for speaking the truth." She waved her finger at Ruby and her shy sister. "Their father ran bootleg whiskey. A common gangster. The mob gunned him down in Chicago. And their mother..."

Fury choked Zita. How dare this awful woman insult those dear Gem sisters? They had been the target of hurtful prejudice most of their lives. Pearl's whimpering made Zita's heart hurt. She understood the damage unkind words did and how deep they wounded. As a child, she had been dreadfully hurt by teasing. Being a foundling had left her open to all sorts of snide cruel comments.

Daniel attempted to stare Beatrice down. But she wouldn't be stopped.

"Their mother, an immoral woman, ran this hotel openly for years. Nothing but a brothel." Beatrice gave a snort. "Imagine keeping their mother and father's bodies in the attic all these years. Disgusting."

Ruby stiffened and then lunged at Beatrice. If Daniel hadn't caught Ruby's hand, she might have blackened Beatrice's eye.

A huge part of Zita wished Ruby's fist had connected with Beatrice's eye.

Zinnia charged up. "Floyd, take your wife home. Neither of you are welcome here. Out! Now!" She pointed toward the door.

Unfortunately, Beatrice had a final word. "And you, Daniel Edward, bringing those ruffians to Arbor Vale. Mark my words, our town will suffer. Crime will escalate." She shook a finger at Daniel. "You'll be sorry. Wait and see. You'll definitely be sorry."

"Get out!" Zinnia roared. "You're no longer welcome here or in my beauty shop."

"No loss there," Beatrice huffed. She grabbed her husband's arm, dragging him toward the door. "Come along, Floyd, we should never have come to this cultural sewer."

As the door slammed, the room remained shrouded in a deafening silence. Zita's heart pounded wildly in her chest. The open house had become a disaster. Pearl was weeping openly. Heather had escaped into their apartment. Jim stood nearby glassy-eyed, mouth open. Zinnia wrapped her arms around Pearl to comfort her. Daniel remained by Ruby's side talking quietly to calm her down.

Confused and disoriented, Zita watched the drama play out. Had everyone in her quiet little community gone crazy in recent months? When did this chaos become an ordinary day in Arbor Vale?

Then that dear caterer, Carl, saved the day. He led a parade of wait staff, carrying fresh trays of goodies to the tables. The remaining guests stampeded toward the food. The confrontation forgotten. *Bless that man.*

Just when Zita assumed things couldn't disintegrate further, Jodie Chatwyn walked in. Jodie, the daughter of the fish crib murder victim, Clive Chatwyn. And she walked straight for Jim.

Zita barely controlled her protective impulse to rush toward her son. She hadn't spoken to Jodie since her father disappeared. The young woman had left town to attend college. Rumors had circulated that Jodie had been married then divorced. As far as Zita knew, Jodie became an English teacher. After being hired last fall at the local high school, she returned to Arbor Vale due to her mother's ill health.

When Jim spotted Jodie, surprise flooded his expression. The surprise melted into a warm, welcoming, open-armed hug.

"Girlfriend, who is that pretty little thing hitting on your son?" Zinnia twittered. "They act as though they know each other *very* well." She handed Zita a dessert plate with two double-chocolate petit fours. "I saved you a couple of treats. This crowd is gobbling them up."

"Thank you. I haven't had a chance to snag any of Carl's treats." Zita accepted the plate. She remained watchful of her son and Jodie. With the discovery of Clive's body, any contact with his family might cause unwanted gossip. She took a bite of the mini chocolate cake. The rich frosting caused her taste buds to tingle. "Carl has certainly outdone himself once again," she said between tiny moans of pleasure.

Zinnia poked Zita on the arm. "That girl, who is she? Jim and she are hunkered down together and closer than two peas in a pod."

A wave of apprehension roared through Zita. Zinnia wouldn't stop questioning without being given an answer. Jim and Jodie were together this afternoon. And that would cause all the old rumors to be dredged up again. Zinnia and her gossip central beauty shop would enjoy this tidbit.

Another poke, harder this time. "Are you listening, Zita?" Zinnia demanded. "Who is that young woman?"

Enjoying the last bit of petit four, Zita chose her words carefully. Fortunately, Zinnia hadn't recognized Jodie yet. "An old school friend of Jim's."

"What's her name?"

Stalling and keeping her answers simple, Zita hoped her friend would either get distracted or change the subject. "That's Jodie."

"Jodie?" Zinnia regarded her with a critical squint. Shocked surprise erupted and she gripped Zita's arm, squeezing hard. "Do you mean Jodie Chatwyn?"

"Unfortunately, yes."

"That isn't good," Zinnia said in a choked voice. "She shouldn't be here talking with Jim. This will cause a mountain of destructive gossip. Her father murdered and in *your* fish crib. Jim helped build that crib." Her cheeks grew pink. She waved her hands as she talked. "Oh my, Jim had all that trouble with Clive. Trouble because of Jodie. That happened right before Clive went missing."

Zita attempted to block out Zinnia's rant. She struggled to find a way to shush her friend. But that never worked with Zinnia. Zita feared she wouldn't quiet down and everyone in the room would realize Jim's connection to Jodie Chatwyn.

Fortunately the open house was beginning to wind down. "I can't talk now," Zita whispered to her friend. "My guests are leaving."

"Yes, but we *will* talk later," Zinnia stated firmly.

Zita walked to the door, leaving her curious friend behind. She thanked people for coming. The newly remodeled hotel generated many positive comments about how her hotel would revitalize the downtown area. A few friends offered support for Daniel's plan for helping at-risk city kids. These remarks delighted Zita, reaffirming her decision regarding all the hard work and money poured into the project.

There were only a few stragglers remaining in the lobby when Zita noticed Heather reappear. After scowling in Jim's direction, she moved purposefully across the room. Zita attempted to ignore the situation by hugging the Gem sisters as they scooted out the door together.

Zita noticed that Zinnia had moved nearer to Jim and Jodie. *Eavesdropping?* Jim introduced Jodie to his wife. Heather continued to glare at him.

Zita wondered what had happened to her placid little life. She had been a lonely widow. Now Kimmy and her baby lived with her and operated a bed-and-breakfast. Her son and daughter-in-law were broke, back in town, and dependent on her. She had inherited the Arbor Vale Hotel along with the Gem sisters. All these things happened in less than a year. And that wasn't counting the murders.

"How exactly do you know Jodie?" Heather's voice echoed across the lobby.

Unable to tolerate any further conflict, Zita left the lobby, stepping out into the afternoon sunshine. She lifted her face to the sunlight, letting it penetrate and warm her. Walking to her car, someone from the hotel called her name. She refused to turn back.

CHAPTER FOUR

Saturday afternoon Zita slunk out of Zinnia's beauty shop. She didn't want to be seen by any of her friends. At least not yet. Wearing one of Zinnia's flamingo-pink smocks was bad enough. But when Zinnia selected a short curly cotton-candy-pink wig for Zita to wear in the parade, it pushed Zita toward ultimate humiliation. The wig only added to the absurdity of her costume. "Why do I let Zinnia lasso me into doing these things? I need to grow a backbone and stand up to her. Yeah, like that's ever going to happen," she grumbled.

She worked her way through the side streets until the town parking lot came into view. All the parade entrants were lining up. She carefully carved a path through the maze of floats and marching units. Up ahead she spotted the pink balloons and paper flowers adorning the beauty shop float. "Exactly when did I volunteer to become part of this bouquet of pink? And I have to stop talking to myself."

Off to the side, Zita noticed Jodie Chatwyn talking with a woman in a wheelchair. *Is that Suzanne?* The change in the woman astonished Zita. Clive's wife had always been slender, but now her face was drawn and tinged with yellow. *Cancer?*

Jodie raised her voice, waving her arms. Zita slipped behind a float, hoping to hear their conversation. Something might be said which would offer a clue about why Clive's body had been disposed of in her fish crib.

A man gripped the handles of the wheelchair, frowning at Jodie. He leaned forward, resting one hand on Suzanne Chatwyn's shoulder. The gesture seemed comforting as well as supportive.

Zita recognized something familiar in the man's appearance. He wore a dark blue and tan flannel shirt, and jeans. His short, dark hair held a mixture of gray. More salt than pepper. His sun-weathered complexion had deeply carved wrinkles with a scar running along his right jawline.

Kenneth Hardgrave. She hadn't seen him in town for several years. After returning from the Vietnam War back in the late sixties, he became reclusive. He built a tepee on his family's land. Zita had heard he lived there for a few years with his Alaskan malamute. Eventually, he built himself a log cabin, living off the land and doing odd jobs for people.

Suzanne covered her face with her hands. Jodie knelt down beside her mother, hugging her gently.

Embarrassed about witnessing the private emotional scene, Zita moved away, continuing on toward Zinnia's float. She recalled a rumor involving Clive Chatwyn and Kenneth Hardgrave. There had been a violent flare-up between them. Something to do with Kenneth hunting out of season.

The high school band started to play a spirited march, hurrying Zita along. Arriving at the float, she found Ruby and Pearl Gem ensconced under pink hair dryers. When they spotted Zita, the sisters waved. Zita saw another elderly client of Zinnia's, Mabel something or other, seated under a third dryer. Mabel was a resident of The Penny Place. The chairs faced in alternating directions, allowing the crowds on both sides to receive candy from the ladies.

Zinnia, in her copper-penny colored wig, had taken her place in the pink convertible pulling the float. "Did you get lost, girlfriend?" she shouted.

With a wave of her hand, Zita acknowledged Zinnia without replying. She climbed the steps to the platform and greeted Mabel and the Gem sisters. She barely had time to position herself next to a wooden counter when organizers shouted directions. The float lurched forward. Zita gripped the edge of the counter with both hands.

"The candy! Get the candy!" Zinnia yelled, waving and pointing.

Zita saw several large pink plastic tubs under the counter. Removing the lid from the nearest container, Zita discovered mounds of wrapped candy. Each wrapper had been imprinted with the name of Zinnia's beauty shop. Her friend definitely grasped the concept of marketing. Zita maneuvered one tub of candy across the platform to Ruby and Pearl. They were able to reach in and toss the treats to the children along the parade route. Returning for another container, Zita tugged and shoved this one next to Mabel.

Zita lifted the final candy tub onto the counter. She would be able to throw the treats and hang on tight.

As the high school band led off the parade, marching music echoed through the street. Their float picked up speed.

Zita noticed Mabel was eating some of the candy. *The older we get the more sweets we crave.*

The parade route would cover eight blocks, passing the Doctor Kate Museum on Second Avenue and ending in front of the big penny monument on the corner of Third Avenue. Zita enjoyed the excitement of the crowd and the laughter of the children.

When they passed the Arbor Vale Cafe, Pearl screamed. Startled, Zita turned. Pearl and Ruby both were pointing at Mabel. The woman had fainted, sliding from her chair onto the floor of the float. Panic stricken, Zita staggered forward. The platform rocked and bounced under her feet.

"Zinnia, Stop! Stop the float!" she shouted. "Help! We need a doctor! Call an ambulance!"

The float jerked to stop, tumbling Zita to her knees next to Mabel. Leaning forward, she touched Mabel's pale and clammy cheek. Zita noticed a silver bracelet on Mabel's wrist.

"Is she dead?" Pearl whimpered. "Has all this excitement been too much for her?"

"Calm down, sister," Ruby interrupted. "Mabel's diabetic. She may have eaten too much of the candy."

Zita read the words on the bracelet. *Diabetic? Is this a diabetic coma?* An ambulance siren wailed, pulling up next to the float. As two emergency medical technicians climbed up onto the platform, relief poured over Zita.

"Mabel is diabetic," Zita said, her voice shaking. She pointed to the bracelet.

She staggered to her feet, moving back to latch onto the counter once again.

An EMT did a finger-prick blood test on Mabel before administering a shot of insulin. When they lifted Mabel for transport, a flurry of empty candy wrappers cascaded onto the floor. One paramedic observed all the empty wrappers and then the tub of candy. He glared up at Zita. "Why would you allow this elderly diabetic woman access to all that candy?"

"But I didn't know," Zita stammered. "I just saw her bracelet now."

He ignored her, concentrating on Mabel.

Zita's stomach roiled. She fought off the wave of nausea.

The high school marching band continued to play. The rat-a-tat-tat of drums and the deep rhythmical um-papa of their tubas were barely audible above the wail of the ambulance siren.

Zita opened her eyes, relieved to discover Mabel and the ambulance gone. And with them the accusations of her carelessness. The float gave a lurch and rolled forward.

Someone jumped up onto the slow moving platform. *Daniel.* He struggled to maintain his balance. Reaching Zita, he gripped the counter next to her.

"Are you okay?" he asked.

Tears trickled down Zita's cheeks. "They blamed me for Mabel's collapse," she said, pointing to the tub of candy. "Why didn't someone tell me she had diabetes?"

"No one should blame you for what happened." Daniel said. "Someone should have warned both you and Zinnia about Mabel's diabetes. There's always candy in these parades." He eyed the scattered candy wrappers. "You've had a shock. Let me help you over by Ruby and Pearl so you can sit down."

Glancing toward the Gem sisters, Zita realized Pearl and Ruby were both upset. They were staring at her, eyes wide and cheeks flushed. She needed to calm them down or there might be another 911 call. *So much for an uneventful little parade in Arbor Vale.*

"Thank you, Daniel; I do need to sit down."

He helped Zita maneuver across the rocking platform. She sank gratefully into a bright-pink salon chair. "Please don't make me use the hairdryer," she begged, shoving the flaming-pink dryer back and out of the way. All this pink reminded her of Pepto-Bismol, which in turn reminded her of her churning stomach.

Pearl tapped Zita on the arm. Her eyes were bright with unshed tears. "Poor Mabel. Is she dead?"

Patting Pearl's hand, Zita consoled her. "Mabel will be fine. The paramedics gave her the insulin she needed." She prayed her words would become fact.

"I'll handle the rest of the candy," Daniel offered, grabbing a handful and tossing the treats to the waiting crowd. Kids scattered, grabbing up every piece. Daniel chuckled, apparently enjoying the candy toss.

Zita wished she could join in. But the responsibility for Mabel continued to weigh heavily upon her. Turning her attention to the pink convertible pulling the float, Zita saw Zinnia still waving to the crowd. Irritation, anger and frustration churned. "Zinnia didn't even come to help with Mabel," she grumbled.

"What did you say, dear?" Pearl asked.

"I'm mumbling to myself," Zita replied.

Pearl smiled happily at Zita as she threw candy to the children. "Such a beautiful sunny day and this is so much fun."

Wishing she could agree, Zita surveyed the crowd. Suddenly alert, from the corner of her eye, she noticed her son standing in the crowd. A woman wearing a baseball cap stood next to him. They were deep in conversation. *Is that Heather?* As if on cue the young woman looked up. Not Heather but Jodie Chatwyn. Again.

As the parade continued past, Zita noticed Heather across the street. Her total attention was focused on Jim and Jodie. If her angry scowl held any indication of what might happen, this definitely wouldn't be good.

Struggling but determined, Zita maintained her composure until the end of the parade. Ruby and Pearl continued to smile and wave to the crowd. Daniel was enjoying the parade, waving and calling out to friends along the route. His rich laughter echoed back across the float. Zita found herself admiring her old friend. As a young man, he had been attractive. But that rugged handsomeness had increased with age. She found herself wondering if his broad shoulders ever tired of the many responsibilities he carried.

Zita scanned the multitude of people milling around the sidewalks. She wondered if Daniel's first group of campers had arrived and if they were at the parade.

The float came to a jerking halt. Relief settled uneasily over Zita. She needed to go to the hospital to find out Mabel's condition. And she needed to deal with her dear friend Zinnia. Why didn't she help with the Mabel fiasco?

Still smiling, Daniel walked across the float, joining the women. "I'll help you ladies down. Miss Ruby and Miss Pearl, I'd be happy to walk you home. The crowds can be a little overwhelming." He turned to Zita. "How are you? I need to make sure Ruby and Pearl get home safely. But I'll come back and we can visit Mabel at the hospital."

Once again, Daniel's caring and kindness became evident to Zita. He apparently understood exactly what she was planning to do. A little frightening that someone knew her so well.

Daniel escorted Ruby and Pearl from the platform. As he passed Zita, he said quietly, "I saw Jim and Heather in the crowd. They're certainly old enough to start treating their marriage and each other with love and respect."

"I wish I saw evidence of that happening," Zita said.

"Daniel, you don't need to fret over us," Ruby said. "Pearl and I plan to meet some friends for coffee and pie at the Arbor Vale Cafe."

Once Daniel assisted the sisters safely from the float, he returned to help Zita down the few steps to the pavement. Immediately a shrill voice accosted them, slicing across her nerves. Beatrice Torkel.

"Officer, Officer, this is the man I want you to talk to," Beatrice ranted, pulling her husband, Floyd, along in her wake, like a tugboat under full steam.

The police officer looked shopworn and weary. The Torkels had that effect on people, especially Beatrice. Zita didn't recognize the officer. The town occasionally brought in extra security during special events.

"What's this about?" Daniel asked.

Without giving anyone else a chance to speak, Beatrice continued spouting. "This is your fault entirely, Daniel Edward. Those boys. Those delinquent boys you brought to our town. During the parade, they burglarized our store. I want them arrested and our money returned."

"Excuse me, ma'am," the officer interrupted. "This is a police investigation. I'm here to speak with Mr. Edward at *your request*. Slander is also a serious offense. I will ask the questions."

Beatrice gave a humph of displeasure, taking a step back and scowling.

Frustration and anger ripped through Zita. *Obnoxious woman.* Who would burglarize Beatrice and Floyd's business, Torkel's

Treasures, during the parade? Warning bells clanged loudly in her head. Too loudly. She massaged her temples, hoping to ward off a headache that had threatened the moment Zinnia sculpted this wig for her. Not to mention the resulting chaos from Mabel's sugar overdose.

Daniel didn't need these accusations the first day of his special weekend camp. An adult chaperone must have been with the boys during the parade.

"Ms. Torkel insisted I question you concerning the boys you brought to Arbor Vale for the weekend," the officer said. "She believes they are responsible for the break-in. I will need to question them with a parent or guardian present."

Daniel turned to Beatrice and Floyd and said, "I hope you didn't suffer too much damage or loss. And please believe me, these young boys did not commit this crime."

"How could you possibly be aware of that, Daniel Edward?" Beatrice attacked again. "Where were you? Certainly not taking your responsibility seriously. I saw you on Zinnia's float, laughing and throwing candy."

"What's the hubbub?" Zinnia asked, joining the group gathered at the rear of her float. She linked arms with Zita.

Beatrice spewed her accusations again. "Daniel's delinquents broke into our antique store and stole several thousand dollars from our cash register." Floyd hid behind his wife, his lips pressed tightly together. Droplets of moisture clung to his pudgy cheeks.

"Ms. Torkel, I've warned you once, there are penalties for slander," the officer stated firmly.

The officer's words silenced Beatrice's, but her expression grew hard and resentful.

Thousands of dollars? Zita bit down hard on her lip. She couldn't believe they had that much money in their register. Maybe in a really good week, but more likely a month's receipts. Zinnia stiffened next to her.

"Oh, my, Beatrice, were you in the store when this happened? Thousands of dollars, you say? Wow! When did your inventory contain anything that valuable to sell? How fortunate they didn't hurt you." Zinnia's voice oozed with sarcasm, mocking Beatrice. "Maybe the officer needs to check your sales receipts to make sure of the exact amount stolen."

Zita gave her friend's arm an encouraging squeeze. *You go, Zinnia.*

Beatrice's cheeks flushed scarlet. "Watch your tone, Zinnia Winwood," she warned. "This isn't any of your business. And I'll check my own receipts."

Stepping between the women, Daniel intervened. "Officer, we can all go to the hotel and straighten this out. I'd like the Torkels to meet the boys visiting us for the weekend."

Floyd continued to crouch behind his wife. The comb-over to hide his baldness flapped in the wind. He tugged at the collar of his shirt.

"Are you coming with us, or staying with Zinnia?" Daniel asked Zita.

Zita didn't want to spend any more time around the Torkels. Besides, she still had to settle the Mabel issue with Zinnia. "Staying. I need to check on Mabel."

The officer, Daniel, and the Torkels snaked their way through the crowd, disappearing from sight.

"Girlfriend," Zinnia said, "Beatrice gives me the heebie-jeebies."

Zita burst out laughing. The laughter released some of the tension this day had caused. Tears rolled down her cheeks.

Zinnia, eyes widened. "What's with you?"

"I love you, Zinnia. You are the best medicine in the world. Heebie-jeebies, indeed. I couldn't have described her effect on people better myself."

"Torkels. Their name should be Trouble Makers." Zinnia lips puckered in disgust. "We should get to the hospital and see how dear Mabel is doing." A flush crept into her cheeks. "I'm really sorry you were left to deal with Mabel's collapse."

Zita couldn't release her frustration that quickly. She cringed, looking at the empty wrappers scattered across the float platform. "Why didn't you come help me with her?"

"I'm truly sorry. By the time I saw what had happened, the ambulance blocked my car door." Zinnia patted Zita's arm. "Mabel's been diabetic for years. Nothing like this has ever happened. I certainly didn't expect her to go into some sort of sugar frenzy today."

Zita realized her friend couldn't be blamed for what happened to Mabel. "I'll feel better once we've learned her condition." She removed the flamingo-pick smock and pulled the wig off her sweaty head.

"Girl, maybe you better leave that on. You have a major hair disaster happening. That's a combination of bed-head and hat-hair."

"Don't care," Zita grumbled. "That thing is hot and itchy." She ran her fingers through her hair, pushing wayward strands behind her ears.

Chuckling, Zinnia took the wig and smock, shoving them into her oversized glossy pink purse. "Cousin, you are a hopeless case. Someday, I'll trick you into a makeover."

The image of a frizzy pink hairdo caused Zita to wince. *Never going to happen as long as I can outrun you.* Linking arms with her friend, they walked the few blocks to the hospital.

"The time has come for us to put our investigation hats on again. Those Torkels need to be taken down," Zinnia said, clamping her jaw tight and thrusting out her chin.

Beatrice and Floyd were more than an irritation. This burglary being blamed on Daniel's campers seemed odd. There were hundreds of visitors in town for the Penny Parade. The Torkels would do or say anything to hinder Daniel opening his camp.

"What's going on with the Clive Chatwyn murder?" Zinnia asked. "Why aren't you working on solving it? Especially since your family is involved." Once Zinnia started off on one of her tangents, she couldn't be turned off.

"My family is not involved, "Zita insisted, wishing she knew that for a fact. "Roger is working the case. He tends to react negatively to our interference. When we get involved, things usually end badly. Very badly."

Zinnia stopped short, jerking Zita to a halt. "Girlfriend, we've been spectacular crime solvers this past year. I'm sure the police wouldn't have solved any of those murders without our help."

"Right. And in the process, we've both almost been killed. I'm not getting involved this time," Zita stated firmly, continuing on toward the hospital.

Zinnia kept on. "What's going on with your Jim and that Jodie Chatwyn? As the saying goes, they appear to be as thick as thieves. Oops, poor choice of words. I saw them together again at the parade. Could they have been involved in Clive's murder?"

Zinnia's accusation spoken out loud filled Zita with a frightening sense of foreboding. Over the years Clive had threatened and alienated half the town of Arbor Vale. Those threats had included her son. Her husband would have done anything to protect Jim. Anything.

Relief had settled over their community when Clive vanished. She wondered if anyone had seriously searched for or even missed him. That included his wife and daughter.

"Girlfriend, are you still with me?" Zinnia demanded. "With that worried look on your face, I'd give more than a penny for whatever is swirling around inside that overheated brain of yours."

"Please, Zinnia, stop. I've had *enough* drama today."

The automatic doors to the hospital emergency room swished open. Coming in from the bright sunlight into the dimly lit reception area caused Zita to pause. Hushed silence and antiseptic smells assaulted her senses. Hospitals brought a flood of unhappy memories.

"Auntie," Kimmy called softly, erasing Zita's sad recollections.

Kimmy stood at the entrance to the waiting room. She held

Kyla on her hip. "I assumed I'd meet you and Zinnia here."

"Oh my goodness," Zinnia gushed. "Your daughter gets cuter every day. I bet she'll be walking soon."

Kyla waved her arms and leaned toward Zita. Zita lifted the baby from her niece's arms.

Kimmy pointed toward a middle-aged couple seated nearby. "This is Mabel's daughter and son-in-law."

Embarrassed, Zita apologized for Mabel's collapse. "I'm so sorry. I wasn't told that your mother was diabetic. How is she?"

"Please," the woman interrupted. "This isn't your fault. Mother is going to be fine. I expect they will be releasing her soon."

Relief threaded across Zita's frayed nerves. "I'm so thankful."

"We've noticed Mom getting confused lately," Mabel's daughter continued. "Normally, she's very strict with her diet. For her safety and our sanity, we'll be moving her in to live with us. This event made that decision easier."

A doctor came out of the ER. He informed Mabel's family that they were releasing her.

After expressing a polite, "Nice meeting you," and "We're thankful Mabel is fine," the trio of women, plus one baby, left the hospital.

"I going back to the beauty shop," Zinnia announced. "Where did you park?"

"The lot by the weekly lumberjack show," Zita said. The strain of the day left her exhausted and dreading the six-block walk to her car.

"Auntie, let me carry that heavy baby bundle."

Zita gladly transferred Kyla to Kimmy's waiting arms.

After saying good-bye to Zinnia outside her shop, they continued on past the hotel. Uneasy, Zita peered around. All was quiet, no sign of the troublemakers. She couldn't handle another confrontation with the Torkels or her son and daughter-in-law today.

"Auntie, you're acting tired and stressed. What's wrong?"

Zita sighed deeply. "Annoying troublemakers, and their name is Torkel." Out of the corner of her eye, she saw Kenneth Hardgrave lifting Suzanne Chatwyn from her wheelchair. Gently placing her in the front seat of his car, he kissed her cheek. "And let's not forget Clive Chatwyn's murdered body in my fish crib."

CHAPTER FIVE

Sunday afternoon, Zita relaxed in her living room, reading the newspaper. The bright May sunshine, coming through the picture window, warmed the entire room. Their bed-and-breakfast guests had checked out. Kimmy and Kyla were out with Roger Brooks and his son, Carter. Kimmy and Roger's relationship continued to thrive, which pleased Zita.

Daniel's first youth retreat at the hotel had ended after lunch. The boys were completely cleared of suspicion for the burglary at Torkel's Treasures when the police were given permission to inspect their luggage. Thankfully, they found nothing. Beatrice Torkel's attempts to cast suspicion on those young boys had totally failed. But it appeared nothing would stop her from attempting to discredit Daniel.

In spite of Beatrice's vicious accusations against the campers, the first weekend had been a success. Daniel had called to tell Zita that a local fishing guide had taken the group out on his pontoon boat. Everyone had a wonderful time and learned to recognize the different types of fish in area lakes. There were opportunities to observe wildlife: eagles, deer, and even a family of otters. And the highlight had been a shore lunch eating the fish they had caught.

Two girls around the age of nine would be coming the next weekend with a counselor from their home church. Daniel shared how much Jim had enjoyed having the youngsters at the hotel.

That comment gave Zita a twinge of disappointment. She'd never experience the joy of grandchildren. Jim and Heather had never seemed interested in having children. Kyla would have to fill that place in her heart. But she grieved for her son and daughter-in-law. They were missing out on one of life's greatest joys.

The ringing phone jarred Zita. Reaching across to the end table, she answered on the second ring.

"Hi, Mom. Could you come by the hotel this afternoon?"

"Jim, is everything okay?" Had something happened? Her shoulders slumped as she glanced around her quiet living room, the unread newspaper in her lap.

"I need to talk with you. I can't leave the hotel."

Zita heard Jim's muffled voice speaking to someone. "Mom, I have to go. A guest needs assistance."

"Jim, I can come to the hotel now. I'll be there in a few minutes." Zita hung up the receiver and rubbed the bridge of her nose. Her first quiet afternoon in such a long time, interrupted. Why did her son need her this afternoon? What problem had arisen now?

After leaving a note for Kimmy, Zita drove to the hotel. Jim met her at the door. "I'll be with you in a minute, Mom." He motioned toward a couple standing at the reception desk. "I have one more checkout. Why don't you wait in the apartment?"

Zita walked toward the back of the lobby. She couldn't shake the feeling that something had happened. Something that Jim didn't want to discuss on the phone. Waiting made her anxious.

As she entered the apartment, she heard the woman at the reception desk remark, "This is a charming historic hotel. It's as though we've stepped back in time. I almost expected there to be gangsters and loggers roaming the halls." The woman giggled. She lowered her voice. "I understand the hotel has quite a colorful past, a brothel." She cleared her throat nervously. "Well, we've enjoyed our stay and will certainly be back again."

Hearing such a positive comment made all the hard work and dedication during the restoration worthwhile. Zita believed in recycling, and that's what had been accomplished. The old hotel had been recycled into a landmark and point of pride for Arbor Vale. She hoped the hotel's success wouldn't hinge on its shady past.

The arrangements for the guests and the weekend campers worked out exceptionally well. The young people spent their days enjoying outdoor activities. They returned later in the evening to the hotel, tired and ready to sleep. There hadn't been a hint of disruptive noisy behavior.

Pouring a cup of coffee, Zita inspected the kitchen. The apartment, even with all modern appliances, still maintained a cozy, vintage northern-Wisconsin decor. She settled comfortably into an oak spindle-backed chair at the kitchen table, listening to the chatter of the departing guests.

Jim bounded into the room, grinning. "Mom, this is exciting. We were filled all weekend, and reservations have been pouring in."

Since Jim and Heather had arrived in Arbor Vale, her son was happy. *If only Heather...* Zita couldn't finish that thought.

Jim reached into a cabinet and removed a small vase with three yellow roses. He walked to the table, placing them in front of Zita. Leaning over, he kissed her cheek. "Happy Mother's Day, Mom."

With all that had happened during this busy weekend, Zita had forgotten the date. She gently touched the soft petals. "Thank you, Jim. They're beautiful. My favorite color."

"I know," Jim said. "Dad always brought you yellow roses. And not only for special occasions. He knew they made you happy."

Tears slowly found their way down her cheeks. Memories of Lorman still had the power to make her heart hurt. Yellow roses would always remind her of his gentle, loving ways.

Jim sat down next to Zita. "Mom, I'm sorry. I didn't mean to upset you."

She dabbed at her eyes. "You didn't upset me. These are happy tears from all the good memories." In an attempt to control her emotions, she changed the subject. "Where is Heather this afternoon?"

"That's one of the reasons I called and invited you over. I couldn't leave the hotel and I wanted to talk privately with you." He stared down at the tabletop. "Things between us keep getting worse. Heather's shut me out and her health has me worried. She's not eating or sleeping normally. No matter what I say, she starts to cry." His hand clenched and unclenched. "Would you talk with her?"

Zita's motherly instinct wanted to fix everything. Age and experience had taught her some hard lessons. Not everything could be fixed. Particularly life. In this case, Heather would not appreciate her interference. "I'm not sure that's the best idea."

Jim's eyes filled with pain. "I love Heather. But I've run out of hope where our relationship is concerned."

"Okay, I'll speak to her," Zita said. As soon as the words hit the air, she wanted to snatch them back.

"Soon? Tomorrow?" Jim asked.

"Tomorrow?" Zita laced her fingers tightly together in her lap. "I have a doctor's appointment in the morning for my yearly physical. I'll talk with Heather later in the day."

"Thanks, Mom." He leaned back in his chair. "Heather will respond to you."

Zita hated to disappoint her son. She expected Heather would respond. But not in the way Jim hoped. This new responsibility thrust upon her became an added burden.

Taking a drink of coffee, Zita was able to regain her composure. She and her son were alone. Now she could ask the questions that were troubling her. She cleared her throat. "Jim, I don't mean to pry...but I saw you with Jodie Chatwyn at the parade." She stirred uneasily in her chair. "With the discovery of her father's body in our fish crib, is it wise for you to be around her?"

A flush slid up Jim's neck. "Yes, we're still friends. I have nothing to hide about our relationship, past or present. And I hope you believe I had nothing to do with Clive Chatwyn's death."

Zita's response didn't come quick enough. Her neck and cheeks grew hot. "Of course I don't believe you had anything to do with Clive's murder."

A muscle tensed in his jaw. "Right. And my relationship with Jodie is private."

Zita started to protest.

"I'm sorry, Mom. But I won't discuss Jodie or her family with you." Without another word, he left the kitchen.

Zita remained at the table, shaken and confused by her son's words. When a murder placed her family under suspicion, she didn't like the idea of private confidences—past or present.

※✕ ✕※

Monday morning, Zita had her yearly physical at the clinic. The doctor surprised her with the results of her usually-dismal cholesterol test. For the first time in years, her levels were normal. Even the dreary day couldn't dampen her spirits. She wanted to skip to the car and then get something buttery and decadent to eat.

When she opened her car door, Zita glanced at the person sitting in the car next to her. Heather. And she was crying. Jim's uneasiness over his wife might be valid. She must be ill. Why else would she be at the clinic?

Fear almost made Zita flee. All the problems solved and unsolved in recent months threatened to overpower her. Could she handle more difficulties?

Without allowing time to change her mind, Zita turned, reaching for Heather's car door. At that instant, Heather noticed her. Intense astonishment and fear flooded her expression. She wiped at the tears on her cheeks. She locked the doors, started the car, and backed out of the parking spot.

Heather's behavior shocked Zita. She jumped away from the moving car. What had caused Heather's erratic actions? Her reaction to Zita had been alarming. *Does she dislike me that much?*

Zita's cell phone chimed. Still shaken by Heather's odd behavior, she frantically rummaged through her purse. The chiming became more annoying. Finally, success.

"Hello. Yes, Kimmy, I'm finished at the clinic."

"Auntie, I have Kyla with me at the hotel. I wondered if you'd be able to stop by and help us clean rooms and do laundry? Cousin Jim is going a little crazy here alone."

"I'm on my way, kiddo." Zita flipped the phone shut. "I'm getting too old for all this physical and emotional stuff." She let out a long sigh. "So much for that buttery and decadent treat."

❀⤙ ⤚❀

A rain shower began spattering on the drive to the hotel. A flash of lightning zigzagged across the cloud-blackened sky. As Zita ran for the hotel door, a sharp crack of thunder made the ground tremble.

Once inside, she removed her damp sweatshirt. From upstairs came the sound of Kyla crying. Zita hurried up the staircase.

Kimmy stood in the hallway, bouncing Kyla on her hip, cooing comforting words to her little daughter.

"What happened?" Zita asked.

Before Kimmy could answer, Kyla turned to Zita and held out her arms. The baby's tears turned off in an instant.

"The storm frightened her," Kimmy explained. "She was content in the playpen until that last bolt of lightning hit."

They heard the bell ding on the reception desk and a shout came from the lobby. "Where is everyone?"

"Sounds like Zinnia." Walking to the top of the staircase, Zita

59

called down, "We're up here. I'm going to help Kimmy with some cleaning and laundry."

Zinnia started up the stairs. "I don't have another appointment at the beauty shop for nearly an hour. I saw your car and decided to stop and offer to help." She spied Kyla. "There's my sweet pumpkin. Let me hold that little angel."

"That's how you can help," Kimmy said. "Auntie is going to help me clean rooms and do laundry. Could you entertain Kyla?"

"Of course," Zinnia gushed. "I'd like nothing better." She regarded the room, giving a shudder. "Beats cleaning hotel rooms."

"Where's Jim?" Zita hoped she wouldn't have to deal with him. He might ask if she had talked with Heather. At least she could answer that question honestly. She certainly hadn't talked with her.

Kimmy stripped the bed of sheets and pillowcases. "Jim's in the apartment, working on the bookkeeping. He promised to help in half an hour."

Zita was relieved at having a short reprieve from facing more of his questions. Kimmy carried the load of laundry downstairs and Zita continued dusting the furniture.

Zinnia carried Kyla to the window, cooing and babbling. Kyla was fascinated by the raindrops hitting the windowpane. She reached out, patting the glass with her tiny hands.

"I'm surprised Heather isn't willing to help with the work around here," Zinnia commented. "You've put a roof over their heads and given Jim a job. That girl acts like a snooty, selfish snob."

Zita concentrated on her dusting, trying to come up with a polite reply. Maybe appearances were deceiving. The image of Heather crying in the clinic parking lot surfaced. "Heather has been through a lot these past months. We need to have patience and understanding."

"That road goes both ways," Zinnia huffed.

Kimmy walked into the room with an armload of clean

bedding.

Jim followed, carrying a stack of towels. "Heather's home. She asked if you were here, Mom, and would like to talk with you privately in the apartment." His voice held a note of hope.

An uneasy dread of facing Heather settled heavily upon Zita. This meeting could be about so many things and none of them good. Yet another disappointment for her son.

Zita left the bedroom, dreaming of a long vacation. Somewhere quiet. A place without dead bodies in fish cribs. Or angry daughters-in-law who might be ill. She pictured a small remote village in Alaska. One of those places without an access road. The only way in would be by plane or boat.

Reaching the lobby, her steps slowed. She lifted her chin defiantly. *I'm going in.*

Heather sat at the kitchen table. There were no tears now. She motioned for Zita to come in. "Please close the door and sit down."

Following Heather's instruction, Zita shut the door to the lobby. She took a seat opposite Heather at the table and clasped her hands tightly together in her lap. She sat silently, waiting for Heather to speak. In recent weeks, her daughter-in-law had become pale and thinner. The silence lengthened.

Heather studied Zita for a long minute. "I wanted to talk with you concerning what happened at the clinic this afternoon," she said. She kept her voice low but the words were curt.

Zita realized there would be no questions allowed and if asked, probably no answers would be given.

"Have you mentioned seeing me at the clinic to Jim?"

Heather visibly relaxed when Zita said, "No."

"Good. I hope you'll respect my privacy and not mention anything to anyone. Do I have your promise?"

"Yes. Of course," Zita responded. She reached across the table, hoping to offer comfort to her daughter-in-law. "If there is anything I can do or if you need to talk with someone?"

Heather stiffened and jerked back. "This is none of your

business." She stood and walked toward the bedroom without another word.

Hurt by Heather's dismissive attitude, Zita sat quietly for a few minutes to gather her emotions. Once again, she had been placed in an awkward situation. Jim would be waiting upstairs to be told the result of this meeting. What could she possibly tell him?

The faint sound of a buzzer interrupted her. The dryer cycle had finished in the basement laundry room. This she could handle. There wouldn't be any drama connected to taking sheets out of the dryer. Escaping the apartment, she fled to the basement, seeking a quiet place to reflect on her conversation with Heather.

The rhythmic swishing of the agitator in the washing machine calmed Zita as she folded and straightened the sheets, pillowcases, and towels. What could she tell Jim? He would certainly ask about her conversation with Heather.

Footsteps sounded coming down the stairs. Zita cringed. Her son carried a huge armload of bedding, which he dropped into a wheeled cart near the washer.

"Mom, why did Heather want to talk with you?"

Zita stopped folding. "Jim, I'm not comfortable sharing private conversations. I'm sorry. I want Heather to realize she can trust me."

She detected movement behind Jim on the stairs. A shadowy figure moved closer. *Heather?* Her daughter-in-law offered Zita a tentative smile, the first indication Zita had received of acceptance or approval from Heather. She may have passed some sort of test.

"I understand, Mom." A frown settled into Jim's features. "But I expected more help from you."

Zita wanted to shout, "More help? You married someone I'd never met, then vanished from my life for over ten years and expect me to fix everything in a month?" She clamped her lips shut to prevent the angry words zipping through her from escaping. She noticed Heather had quietly fled. "*You* need to find a way to talk with *your* wife. Love your wife, son. Heather has been through many changes these past months. Patience, time, and love solve most problems. Mostly love."

Embarrassment flickered across his face. "I'm sorry, Mom. You're right. You've done so much for us. And I am grateful. But Heather and I need to resolve our issues together. As they say, I need to man up."

Exactly. "The longer problems exist in a relationship the harder they are to solve."

Before he left the basement, Jim hugged his mother. Zita returned to loading the washer and dryer with bedding and folding the clean sheets. After a few minutes she carried fresh bedding upstairs, joining Kimmy, Zinnia, and Kyla. The trio had moved on to cleaning another room.

When Zita walked in, Kimmy asked, "What did Heather want?"

Zita placed the clean sheets on the dresser. "She wanted to talk. I don't want to make this sound like a secret or mystery, but our conversation is private."

Apparently, Zinnia sensed a juicy piece of gossip. She shifted Kyla against her shoulder. "That does make your meeting sound mysterious."

Staring hard at her friend, Zita reminded her, "Would you like all our conversations made public?"

More color flooded Zinnia's already rosy cheeks. "N-no. Of course not," she stuttered.

"Good. Let's change the subject," Zita said, spreading a fitted sheet on the mattress. "I had a great appointment at the clinic. For the first time ever, my cholesterol level is not off the charts. And I plan to stop and have a hot fudge sundae on the way home."

Kimmy grinned. "What, no chocolate doughnuts?"

"Maybe tomorrow," Zita said, chuckling.

"All this sweet talk is making me hungry." Zinnia checked her watch. "Time to get back to the shop." She kissed Kyla's chubby little cheek and handed her off to Kimmy.

"I'm tired. I'll go home and fix lunch." Kimmy cuddled the baby in her arms. "This young lady is probably hungry too. Then it's time for a nap."

"I'll stay and finish a few more rooms," Zita offered.

"We've done enough for today," Kimmy said. "The hotel won't be full again until the weekend."

Relieved, Zita didn't need to be told twice. She gathered up her things and followed Kimmy and Zinnia down the stairs.

Zinnia hurried off toward the beauty shop. After Kimmy strapped Kyla into her car seat, Zita walked around to the driver's side. Glancing across the street, she noticed a woman standing in the town parking lot. Jodie.

She saw someone step out from behind a parked van. *Jim.* Zita fumbled with her car keys. Her son had made things very plain—his involvement with Jodie had nothing to do with her. She reflected on Heather's struggles and sorrow. Maybe the trouble in their relationship didn't rest with Heather after all. Zita's emotions shifted from aggravation toward her son to sympathy for her daughter-in-law. An icy fear twisted her insides. Were Jim and Jodie involved in Clive's murder?

CHAPTER SIX

Tuesday morning, Kimmy prepared for a new bed-and-breakfast guest who had called the day before and made reservations. She stood at the counter checking her recipe book, with Kyla on her hip. "Her name is Brandy Gardell,"

Zita sat at the kitchen table, finishing her coffee. "Where is she from? And is she coming alone?"

"Coming up from Milwaukee. And yes, she's coming alone. Plans to arrive this afternoon."

Staring down at her cup, Zita could only imagine what Brandy Gardell would be like. She was always a little anxious when a new guest arrived. Since opening the bed-and-breakfast, two guests had tracked evil and murder into her home. The memories slithered down her spine. "Why is she coming to stay with us?"

Starting a fresh pot of coffee, Kimmy said, "Not a clue. But I'm almost finished cleaning the downstairs room and planning tomorrow's breakfast for her. I'd like to help Jim at the hotel this morning, if I have time."

Pausing to mentally run through her day, Zita decided she had time to help. "Why don't you stay here and welcome our guest. I'm caught-up on my silhouette and woodcraft orders. I'll work at the hotel for a few hours."

Kyla fussed to get down. Kimmy placed her in the playpen. The baby immediately reached for her favorite stuffed toy, a small white lamb. "Thanks, Auntie, that will help. I'll be relieved when those two local students take over the cleaning and laundry at the hotel for the summer."

June, July, and August would be filled with tourists coming and going. Zita hoped she had the stamina to survive. The first few years after her husband's death had been quiet. Too quiet. Now with each passing year, her life became filled with more and more responsibilities. She had continued the small woodcraft business in her home to supplement her widow's pension. When her niece and baby Kyla arrived last fall, they added the bed-and-breakfast. Another life-changing event occurred when she inherited the hotel from her aunt. Now her son and daughter-in-law had moved back to Arbor Vale and were living at and managing her hotel. Her life kept getting more crowded and complicated.

❀✄ ✄❀

Later that morning, Zita drove to the hotel. She wanted to be back in time to meet their new guest. If any negative feelings surfaced, Brandy could be transferred to the hotel.

Stepping out of her car into the bright warm sunshine lifted Zita's spirits. The air remained crisp and cool. A perfect May morning.

Jim met her at the door. "Good-morning, Mom. I didn't expect you to be here today."

"Kimmy had to prepare for a new bed-and-breakfast guest. I've completed all my projects at home, so I decided to stop by and finish cleaning more rooms this morning."

Jim walked to the reception desk and lifted an armload of fresh sheets. "I'll carry these upstairs. Between last night and early this morning, all the laundry is done."

Her son was tired and drawn, his shoulders drooping. Was this the result of long hours of work and maybe worry over Heather? The harder Zita struggled to ignore her concerns over Jodie Chatwyn, the more they persisted. Could Jim's tiredness be connected to fear of what the police might discover about Clive's murder?

"Two local young women will begin working here part-time on Monday," Jim said. "Jodie has offered to help out once the school year ends. She can't leave her mother for long periods of time. But they can use extra money to help with her mom's medical bills." He paused, waiting for his mother response.

Bringing Jodie into the hotel with Heather was definitely not a good idea. Should she give him the benefit of the doubt? An act of kindness to help an old friend and neighbor? Zita wished she could find the words to shake her son up and make him understand the difficulty of having Jodie in the hotel with Heather. She moved toward the staircase, anxious to escape. "Might be best to discuss this with Daniel and Heather," she answered as casually as she could manage.

"I'll put the towels and bedding in the hall closet, Mom. All the cleaning supplies are in the large cabinets in the bathrooms. If you need anything, give me a shout. I'll be downstairs straightening up the laundry area."

Obviously her son decided not to pursue the Jodie conversation. Did Jim's resemblance to his father end with his physical appearance? Since his return, he seemed to lack the strength of character Lorman had possessed. The weakness she saw troubled her. She wished Lorman were still alive to mentor him. Daniel had filled that role since Jim and Heather had returned to Arbor Vale, but would Daniel's influence be enough?

When Jim started down the staircase, Zita needed to bite down on her tongue to stop herself from asking where Heather was.

For the next two hours, Zita completed the tasks in each

bedroom. When she was dusting the fourth room, she heard footsteps. She stopped dusting and listened.

"Zita, are you here?" an all-too-familiar policeman's voice called.

Peeking out the door, she discovered Roger walking down the hall. "I'm here. What's up?" His serious police scowl caused Zita to grip the edge of the door frame. What had brought him here today? This had to be bad news. Clive news.

"This will only take a few minutes," Roger said. "I have a few more questions. I trust you to answer honestly." He pointed to the small table and chairs in the guest room. "Do you want to sit down?"

"No, obviously this concerns Clive Chatwyn. What can I possibly add to our previous conversations?"

"They have a cause of death," Roger said, his words grating roughly across Zita's nerves.

Zita didn't release her grip on the door frame. She gritted her teeth, waiting to hear the worst.

"The best they can determine is severe head trauma." Roger rocked back on his heels, leaning against the wall. "Let's discuss the time surrounding Clive's disappearance. He apparently made enemies easily. But why your fish crib? "

"Good question. And I don't have an answer. It could simply have been a convenient place for someone to hide the body." She considered Jim and Jodie and their relationship as high school sweethearts.

"Your son and Jodie Chatwyn. Is there something there you need to tell me?" Roger asked.

"You should be asking Jim these questions," Zita hedged.

"I plan to do exactly that, and I expect the truth from you." Roger jammed his hands into his pants pockets and waited silently.

"Okay. Jim and Jodie dated back in high school. After Jim graduated from college that winter, they started dating again. Clive didn't want his daughter dating *anyone*. Kind of creepy.

Lorman and I started noticing Clive at odd times on the lake or near our property. At one point, he threatened Jim to stay away from Jodie."

"Threatened?" Roger interrupted. "How?"

"This is what Jim told us. I didn't hear the threat," Zita explained. "Clive told Jim if he saw Jodie with him again, there might be a fatal accident." She couldn't suppress the anger these memories produced.

"And?" Roger prompted, taking his notebook out.

"And things escalated. Clive made the mistake of approaching my husband. Once again there were threats." The hair on the back of Zita's neck tingled. "Roger, I hated the man. No one threatens my family."

"So you noticed times that Clive was apparently stalking your family." Roger wrote something in his notebook.

"Stalking. Yes, that's exactly what Clive did that winter. The whole time Lorman and Jim built the crib, Clive spied on them. One day he showed up demanding Lorman's permit from the Department of Natural Resources to construct the fish crib. Lorman had registered the fish crib and had the permits. He did everything by the book. I'm sure that annoyed Clive." Zita paused, deciding how much to tell Roger. "Clive spent one morning measuring the logs to make sure the structure met all specifications. Once again he lost any chance of fining us."

"Were there any serious confrontations between Clive and Jim?"

Rubbing a hand across her forehead, Zita had difficulty recalling all the details. So much time had passed. She had been completely occupied in caring for Lorman during his battle with cancer. "We kept a tight watch on Jim around that time. No one could trust Clive and what he might do. He had that kind of reputation. All bad. There wasn't another threat. Jim applied for a job in Illinois and went for an interview, and Clive disappeared. Everyone assumed he had run off with another woman."

"Why another woman?" Roger asked.

"I heard there were other women. Could have only been small-town gossip."

"Any guesses on who he might have been involved with? A name?" Roger tapped his pen on the notebook.

Closing her eyes, Zita tried to pull up a name. "Honestly, Zinnia probably has a list. Rumor is her middle name."

Roger grinned. "So you're saying I have to talk to Zinnia?"

Thoughts of her best friend brought a grin to Zita's lips. "Zinnia will love chatting with you."

"That's what I'm afraid of. Anything else?"

"The day and time the crib sank was a big event. Lorman and I had a bet going. I won and he cooked dinner. Such a great memory. Will the actual date help?" Zita found herself starting to relax.

"Maybe. Did Clive ever actually trespass on your property?"

"Not that we saw. But every time Lorman or Jim went out ice fishing, Clive would show up. He'd inspect their fishing licenses, count the fish they caught, make sure they didn't have too many fishing poles or tip-ups on the ice. Lorman wouldn't leave any fishing equipment unattended for fear Clive would be waiting to fine him."

"Sounds like harassment," Roger said, still taking notes. "Threats, stalking, and harassment. Clive sounds like a real piece of work. All because he didn't want Jim dating his daughter?"

"I've mentioned there is a lengthy list of people who were more than happy when he disappeared." Had she managed to convince Roger that her family couldn't be involved in Clive's murder? Had she convinced herself?

When Roger flipped his notebook closed, Zita's desire to clean any more hotel rooms evaporated. "I need a cup of coffee. If Jim has the pot on in the kitchen, you're welcome to join me."

"Sounds good. To face Zinnia, I might need some caffeine." Roger sounded tired and stressed. He followed Zita down the staircase.

"You're going round and round, questioning the same people.

70

Maybe Zinnia will be able to give you a new lead."

"Did someone mention my name?" a twittery voice called.

As they joined her friend in the lobby, Zita whispered to Roger, "You may have to handle Zinnia without a shot of caffeine."

"I didn't expect to find you here, Roger." Zinnia studied Roger and then Zita. "Have I missed another murder?"

"Not a new murder. Roger is investigating an old one." Today her friend's shoulder-length light brown hair had peach highlights. One of Zinnia's many wigs. Fortunately not her usual self-inflicted beauty shop disaster. Zita looked toward the apartment at the back of the lobby. "Is Jim around?"

"He went to the post office. I passed him on the way in. Told him I'd hang with you until he returned." Zinnia batted her eyes at Roger. "But I didn't expect to find attractive male company." Then she managed to hopscotch on to another topic. "So what's the latest on Clive? Have you arrested anyone yet?"

Poor Roger. Zinnia managed to fluster the poor man. Color flooded his cheeks. When he swallowed hard, Zita saw his Adam's apple bounce. "Good thing you stopped by, Zinnia. Roger has a few questions for you."

"Oh, good. I might even have a few answers. This concerns Clive, right?" Zinnia started to effervesce. "I love being part of these investigations. I'm really good at solving murders."

Zita escaped to the kitchen. The coffee maker had been turned off, the pot empty. "Roger, do you have time for me to make a fresh pot of coffee?"

"Don't bother, Zita. I'm due for a lunch break after this interview." Roger turned his attention back to Zinnia. "Do you remember the names of some of the women who were involved with Clive?"

Zita came back into the lobby, leaning on the reception desk. Any information Zinnia could share with Roger might help clear her family. She saw Zinnia's cheeks turn a delicate shade of pink. What information would Zinnia find embarrassing to share?

"I'd better sit down. This could take a while." Zinnia sank down onto the love seat.

Zita crossed the lobby and sat down next to her friend.

Staring at Roger, Zinnia gripped Zita's hand. "I'd like to start with a disclaimer. I did not kill Clive Chatwyn." She sat up straighter and mumbled, "I wanted to kill him. But that doesn't count as a crime. Half the women in this town wanted him dead."

Startled by Zinnia's scandalous words, Zita said, "You never mentioned having trouble with Clive."

Zinnia squeezed Zita's hand a little tighter. "Honey, when Clive disappeared, Lorman was ill and Jim had left town. You didn't need to hear the sordid details of Clive's escapades."

A bruising memory of that time buffeted Zita. She had become an expert at controlling those agonizing emotions. They slowly subsided into a dull ache, allowing her to refocus on Zinnia's evidence. She leaned back against the cushion, wanting to hear more of Zinnia's story.

Roger slid onto the chair across from the two women. Once again he flipped open his ever-present notebook. "Zinnia, let's start with why you wanted to kill Clive?" He quickly added, "But didn't."

The rosy color in Zinnia's cheeks heightened to scarlet. "That man propositioned me." She gave a disgusted huff. "I'm not that kind of woman. And Clive, a married man with a daughter."

Clive had been mean and vindictive. But his loathsome behavior toward women left a vile taste in Zita's mouth. *Why am I not surprised someone murdered him?*

"When did this happen?" Roger asked.

Stiffening, Zita waited to hear Zinnia's reply.

"Six weeks before he vanished." Zinnia shifted restlessly on the love seat. "I told that sleazy creep exactly what I thought of him. Clive didn't take rejection well."

After adding something to his notes, Roger continued questioning Zinnia. "What happened?"

An angry flush worked into her cheeks as Zinnia said, "He

stalked me, showing up wherever I went."

Zita patted her friend's hand. "I'm so sorry. You should have told me. Were you afraid?"

Zinnia pressed her lips together, her hands balling into fists. "He frightened me at first. Then I got mad."

Knowing what that meant, Zita's lips twitched. She could almost feel sorry for the now-deceased Clive.

"And?" Roger coached.

"I simply confronted him. Told him I had a twelve-gauge shot gun and a 357 magnum revolver. And I wouldn't hesitate to use them. If he continued stalking me, I'd shoot first and then talk to the police." Making eye contact with Roger, Zinnia lifted her chin in a defiant gesture. "I never saw him again."

Zita choked back a giggle. *You go, Zinnia. That's why I want you on my side in any battle.*

Roger stopped writing and looked directly at Zinnia. Zita noted what appeared to be a new respect for her friend in his eyes.

"Were there rumors of Clive leaving town with another woman? Do you know who she might have been?" Roger asked.

Without hesitating, Zinnia said, "Carmela Kream with a K."

"Are you kidding?" Zita asked, adding a giggle.

"No, seriously, that was her legal name," Zinnia insisted.

Continuing to write, Roger mumbled, "Carmela Kream with a K."

"I hired Carmela right out of beauty school. The girl could work magic with hair-- and men. Enter Clive." Zinnia gave an exaggerated shudder. "I warned her but... Carmela picked up her last pay check and quit. Said she had a ticket out of town. I never saw her or Clive again."

A disturbing idea crept into Zita's thoughts. Could there be another body in the lake?

"Any other women? Or angry husbands?" Roger asked.

"You could add Beatrice and Floyd Torkel to your list," Zinnia answered

Zita cringed, hearing the Torkels' name. They enjoyed

causing problems for everyone.

"Now that's a story," Zinnia continued. "Clive took one of his wife's pieces of jewelry into their shop, Torkel's Treasures, to sell. *Took* as in without permission. The necklace had been in Suzanne's family for generations. Beatrice offered him a hundred dollars. Clive snatched that money and went to the nearest bar."

"How is that pertinent to this investigation?" Roger leaned forward, resting his elbows on his knees.

Zinnia grinned. "The Torkels cheated Clive big time. Beatrice recognized quality jewelry. Well, you can imagine what happened when Suzanne discovered her necklace missing. She had insured the piece for several thousand dollars. Clive was viewed as a fool by the whole town for getting swindled by Beatrice."

Zita winced, realizing how Clive would react to being made Beatrice's patsy. "I'm surprised Beatrice didn't end up in my fish crib."

"Suzanne demanded her property back. But Beatrice had already sold the necklace to someone out of state." Zinnia paused, licking her lips as if relishing something tasty. "Now, that was a scandal. Everyone believed Beatrice had falsified her records and squirreled that gorgeous antique necklace away for herself. I never heard if Suzanne located the supposed buyer."

Once again, Zita wondered why she never heard any of this gossip. Of course, Zinnia's beauty shop remained gossip central in Arbor Vale. A place Zita avoided.

"Is there more to this story?," Roger asked.

"Of course there were threats." Enjoying the spotlight, Zinnia preened before continuing. "But everyone waited for Clive to do something sinister. That tied his hands. If anything happened to the Torkels or their business, he would have been blamed. Within a few weeks, Clive was gone and Suzanne never pursued regaining her property. That seemed odd at the time."

Fidgeting, Zita laced her fingers together to calm them. This story left a lot of loose strands, reminding her of one of Zinnia's knitting fiascoes. Obviously, Clive didn't leave town. But who put him in the fish crib? Suzanne because of the necklace? Had there been a violent confrontation with the Torkels? Could the beautician, Carmela Kream be the killer or another victim?

After making a few more notations in his notebook, Roger said. "This has added a few more suspects to the pot. You've been very helpful, Zinnia. Thank you."

Sitting up straighter, Zinnia primped some more, patting at her wig. "I do my civic duty. I've been a big help in previous investigations."

Zita nearly choked, trying not to laugh. Roger's eyes widened with alarm and a hint of dread. Zita could tell he planned to exit quickly before Zinnia insinuated herself into this murder inquiry.

He stood up, inching his way toward the door. "I'll be in touch if I have any more questions."

Watching Roger scurry away, Zita wished she could escape as well.

"That poor man needs our help with this murder." Zinnia shifted restlessly on the love seat. "Time for us to get involved and clear your family of this terrible murder. I can't believe the killer, in effect, dumped the body at your door."

Had someone planned to frame her family for this murder? Zita hadn't considered that possibility. She needed to stop Zinnia or things might get out of hand. "We're not to get involved in these investigations. Our lives have been in danger on more than one occasion."

"Don't exaggerate, girlfriend. There has always been someone on hand to rescue us. I'll start by googling Carmela. Find her, and we might get some answers."

"Zinnia, please don't start googling again."

Zinnia ignored her friend's words. "Then there's those Torkels. I'd like both of them to go down for this murder. Maybe I need to ask Beatrice how that necklace issue ended."

"You shouldn't talk with Beatrice, Zinnia. That might complicate the situation. Please let Roger handle her interrogation."

Zinnia puckered her lips. "Don't spoil all my fun. I have several friends connected with the Department of Natural Resources. I'll find out who is still in the area that worked with Clive. That could be a great lead."

"I hate to drizzle on your parade, sweetie. I'm sure Roger has done that already." *I need to stop her.* "Getting involved before caused you serious injury."

"That was an accident." Leaning in, Zinnia hugged her friend. "I'm talking wives and girlfriends of employees. They're far more willing to splatter their beans."

"Splatter their beans? Don't you mean spill?"

"No. I mean splatter. When those girls let loose with gossip, we're talking splatter. Who knows where their words will land. And on whom."

That's what I'm afraid of. Zita's frustration continued to grow. She resented being put in this situation again. "This murder investigation involves my family. Please, don't do anything to make the situation murkier. Jim has enough going on with the hotel and Heather. I don't want any splatter landing on him." *Or my late husband.*

CHAPTER SEVEN

Zita arrived home, hoping to find peace, quiet, and lunch. Not necessarily in that order. She hoped to have a relaxing meal with Kimmy. Thankfully there weren't any extra cars in the driveway. Their new bed-and-breakfast guest hadn't arrived.

The house was silent and empty. *Odd.* Zita called Kimmy's name. No answer. Then she noticed the note on the counter. Roger had come by and taken Kimmy and Kyla to lunch. Well, she had gotten her wish for peace and quiet. But she hated eating alone.

She rummaged through the refrigerator, examining the leftovers. She discovered a small container of chicken casserole and heated the glass dish in the microwave.

As the microwave beeped, the doorbell buzzed. *Great!* Zita hurried to answer the door. A young woman Kimmy's age stood outside, suitcase in hand.

"You must be Brandy Gardell," Zita welcomed her. "Come in." She opened the door wider.

"And you must be Zita Stillman," the woman replied. "I arrived earlier than I expected. I hope that won't be an inconvenience."

"Not a problem." Zita ushered her into the breezeway. "The room is downstairs." She led their guest down the staircase. Zita had a good first impression of Brandy. The woman lived up to her name. She had her russet-colored hair pulled back into a ponytail. And Kimmy might enjoy the company of someone nearer her own age.

"The private bath is to your right," Zita said, walking Brandy through the apartment. "The bedroom has a separate entrance to the backyard and the lake." Their guest was satisfied with the accommodations.

Zita couldn't help wondering why the woman had come to Arbor Vale. And why she had chosen their bed-and-breakfast. "Once you've settled in, my niece will check with you about breakfast. How long do you plan to stay with us?"

"A few days, a week at the most." She examined the room. "This is a nice apartment, and your view of the lake is incredibly beautiful."

"Thank you."

Zita turned to leave. "I'll be upstairs if you need anything."

"I heard a murder victim was discovered in your lake," Brandy said. Her attention remained on the large picture window overlooking the lake.

Zita didn't respond to this blunt statement. Was Brandy only staying with them because of the murder? Could she be some nosy weirdo? They didn't need another creepy guest staying with them.

Brandy turned, scrutinizing her. "What can you tell me about the murder victim?"

"Why all the questions?" Zita asked.

"Curiosity. I found the newspaper story intriguing." Brandy turned back toward the window.

Zita chose to dismiss Brandy's questions. She returned to the kitchen and her cold lunch.

After reheating the chicken casserole, she sat down at the table. Movement near the lake caught her attention. She walked to the patio door. Brandy was in the yard, snapping pictures of the lake.

The breezeway door closed with a thud. Baby chatter echoed into the kitchen, announcing Kimmy and Kyla had returned home. "Auntie, has our guest arrived early?" Kyla waved her chubby arms excitedly at Zita. "Oh, we've interrupted your lunch. I'll change Kyla and put her down for her nap and then we can talk."

When Kimmy returned to the kitchen, she joined her aunt at the table. "So, tell me what you think of our guest."

"Attractive. Pleasant. Wondering why she's here."

Kimmy giggled. "You're starting to be suspicious of all our guests. They can't all have ulterior motives for staying with us."

"The first thing she asked concerned the murder victim in the lake. I found that odd."

"I'm sure she's only curious." Kimmy said. "Finding Clive after all these years has been in all the newspapers and the main topic of conversation in all the cafes."

"You're right," Zita agreed. "I'm probably getting paranoid."

"We could do what Zinnia does, google her," Kimmy suggested.

"Why don't you meet her first? She might still be out by the lake taking pictures."

Kimmy stood and walked to the patio door. "You're right, she is outside. Good time to meet her." She slipped out the door.

Zita gathered her plate and cup, carrying them to the sink. Maybe Kimmy would get the answers to calm her misgivings. A ceramic mug slipped from her hands, crashing to the floor. By the time Kimmy returned to the kitchen, Zita had finished cleaning up the shattered mess. Her niece's expression was clouded with uneasiness.

"Is there a problem?" Zita asked. Maybe they should stop opening their home to visitors. Their track record left a lot to be desired.

"I'm not sure. At least she's honest and open about her reason for being here."

Uncertainty and caution crept across Zita's nerves. "That doesn't sound good."

"Brandy's a reporter for one of those tabloid papers. The kind that are displayed in the grocery store checkout lane. Something called *The Tattler*. She's here to do a story about the body in the fish crib." Kimmy gave an impatient shrug. "I'm not sure we should allow her to stay."

"That doesn't sound like quality investigative reporting." Zita speculated what repercussions this type of story might have on them. Would they be able to persuade Brandy to stick to the facts and not offer any opinions surrounding the case? "If Brandy stays, we might be able to influence what she writes. The truth is better than some scandalous lies. Besides, who reads that trash?"

"The answer to that," Kimmy said with a giggle, "is way too many people."

"Probably," Zita agreed. "But in this case, we might need to heed the advice and keep our enemies close."

❉〉 〈❉

The next morning, bright sunshine created a cozy atmosphere in the kitchen. When Brandy arrived for breakfast, she stood admiring the view of Arrowhead Lake. "The ripples on the water sparkle like diamonds. Hard to believe that a murder victim lurked beneath the surface all these years."

Zita's mouth tightened to stifle an irritated retort. She pictured Brandy's words as the lead-in sentences to her yet unwritten article. "Please sit down. Breakfast is ready."

Zita poured the coffee and Kimmy arranged plates of scrambled eggs, bacon, and cinnamon apple muffins on the table. Kyla sat in her high chair, munching on Cheerios.

During the meal the women discussed Arbor Vale and Brandy's job as a reporter in Milwaukee. They skillfully avoided the subject of Clive Chatwyn.

"My goal isn't to work for *The Tattler* forever," Brandy said.

"I want to be an investigative journalist. This assignment at the tabloid is my chance for a real career at a respected newspaper or magazine."

Brandy didn't sound like she would write a story filled with half-truths and innuendos. Not if she wanted a job at a reputable publication. As her desire to influence Brandy to report the truth grew, some of Zita's apprehensions subsided.

As they sat back sipping their coffee, Brandy removed a notebook and pen from her purse. "Would you be willing to answer a few questions? I have an appointment with the police later this morning."

Kimmy stood, stacking and removing the dishes from the table. "Would anyone like more coffee?"

Both Zita and Brandy replied, "No."

"I didn't live here at the time of Clive's disappearance," Kimmy said, carrying the plates to the sink. "Never met the man. So I won't be able to answer any of your questions." She returned to the table, lifting Kyla from the high chair. "I have some work to finish at the hotel this morning. I'll see everyone later."

Zita was determined to keep her answers short and factual. She couldn't afford to mention anything that might incriminate her family.

Turning to Zita, Brandy finished jotting down a few notes. "Did you know Clive personally?"

"Only indirectly. He worked locally for the Wisconsin Department of Natural Resources." Zita relaxed. She could handle this.

"Do you have an opinion as to why someone hid his body in your fish crib?"

"Good question." Zita paused, struggling for a reason. "I've thought of nothing else since they found the body. My only answer is opportunity. The crib had been finished and sitting on the ice for several weeks. The murderer might have used it for a convenient spot to dump the body."

"Did your family have enemies? Enemies that would have

81

wanted you blamed for this murder?"

Enemies? Zita didn't like the possibility of more enemies. During the past year, she had gathered quite a few. But the only enemy from that time had been Clive himself. Something she didn't plan to mention to this reporter.

The door banged shut in the breezeway. "Excuse me, I either have a customer or Kimmy forgot something."

Zita had started to stand when Zinnia popped into the kitchen. Her hair a fluffy apricot confection. "Hey, girlfriend. Oops, sorry, you have company or a new guest."

Zita cringed. The interview had been under control. But she could never be certain what her friend might say. "Brandy is our bed-and-breakfast guest. She's a reporter doing a story on the murder. Brandy, this is my best friend, Zinnia."

"Best friend and cousin," Zinnia added, swooping in and sitting down at the table. "Nice to meet you. So you heard that fishermen discovered a body in the lake. Zita and I have been investigating the murder. And I googled Carmela Kream. You'll never guess what I found out."

Teeth clenched, Zita couldn't decide if she should scream, kick, or throw something at Zinnia. Once she started babbling, the words would continue to flow like a raging torrent. Brandy scribbled furiously in her notebook.

"Zinnia, Brandy is a reporter," Zita repeated with a slight shake of her head, hoping Zinnia would understand the significance and clam up. Unfortunately, Zinnia couldn't be stopped.

"Brandy's a reporter, I heard you the first time. That's great. Maybe she can help us uncover the murderer. That would be so much fun. Will I get my name in the paper? My last name is Winwood."

Zita's frustration and aggravation intensified. "Brandy works for a tabloid called *The Tattler*." Would this be a strong enough hint to stop Zinnia's prattle? Still, she didn't want to give the impression that she had something to hide.

"*The Tattler*, I love that paper. We discuss their articles all the time at my beauty shop. In fact, I have a subscription." Zinnia bubbled with joy over this news. "Can you imagine what the girls would say if my name was in that paper?"

Blood pounded in Zita's temples. She had lost this battle. Her stomach knotted. If only she could prevent Zinnia from pointing an accusing finger at Jim or her husband.

"Who or what is a Carmela Kream?" Brandy asked.

"Carmela worked for me but left town when Clive disappeared. I assumed they had run off together." Zinnia giggled and pointed toward the lake. "Apparently not. But it couldn't have happened to a nicer guy."

"Why do you say that?" Brandy continued to take notes.

"I'm sure Zita told you how vindictive and evil Clive was." Zinnia shuddered.

"No, she didn't. I'd love to hear what you remember."

"There were the threats he made to Zita's son, Jim," Zinnia said.

A suffocating sensation tightened Zita's throat. Would Zinnia ever think before she spoke? Was there any way to save this situation? "This happened such a long time ago." Her excuse sounded lame.

"Oh, back to Carmela. She's living in Green Bay and has her own beauty shop now. She could work magic with hair. Of course, that doesn't eliminate her as a suspect in Clive's murder. And I suppose Zita and her family remain suspects." It appeared Zinnia finally realized she had said too much. She jumped up sputtering, "Oh my, the time, I'm late. Isabel is due in to have her roots touched up. Have to run." Shifting from foot to foot, her cheeks flooded with color. She mouthed the word, "Sorry" in Zita's direction. With a springy bounce she bounded out the door.

"Interesting friend," Brandy commented. "Is her beauty shop in town?"

Zita could only manage a nod, waiting for harder questions to follow. Brandy would obviously be paying a visit to the beauty shop. Zinnia, Zinnia, Zinnia, what could anyone do to stop her runaway tongue?

"Do you want to share any more information concerning the murder victim? According to Zinnia, it sounded as though he made more enemies than friends."

"You'll have better luck getting the facts of the case if you keep your appointment with the police," Zita replied, keeping her tone brisk. "Especially if you're interested in becoming an investigative journalist and not some gossipmonger."

Obviously chagrined, Brandy gathered her notebook and slid back her chair. "You're right, I don't want to be late." She stood and hurried out the door.

Zita remained at the table, clasping her hands tightly together to keep them from shaking. Any hope she had of protecting her family from being smeared by Clive's murder now rested with Zinnia and Brandy. That thought was terrifying.

❋⟡ ⟡❋

Later that afternoon, Zita cut life-size wooden silhouettes in her workshop. She worked on the several popular dog designs, especially black labs. They sold as quickly as she cut them. She was never able to keep them in stock.

Through the large picture window, she saw Brandy pull into the driveway. After turning off the jigsaw, she walked into the breezeway to attend to their guest.

As soon as she walked in, Brandy started talking. "Wow! Between the information at the police station and the gossip at the beauty shop, Clive Chatwyn is turning out to be a real piece of work. Sounds to me like half the community would have been happy to dispose of him. This could be my breakout story."

Not the outcome of Brandy's investigating that Zita had hoped for. She wondered what she could do to stem this unwelcome surge of gossip. Roger's often repeated words came to mind, "No comment and ongoing investigation." Now if only she could drum that phrase into Zinnia.

"There's a lot of buzz surrounding the Torkels," Brandy continued. "Clive must have hated them for cheating him. What's your opinion of the burglary at their store?"

Zita had forgotten the break-in at Torkel's Treasures during the Penny Parade. She had difficulty believing Beatrice's claim that several thousand dollars had been stolen. She wouldn't share that information with Brandy.

"You might want to write about Daniel Edward and the small camp he's starting for at-risk city kids. He has been using the Arbor Vale Hotel for small groups and their chaperones. That would also make a good human interest story."

"Right. I'll give that some consideration," Brandy said, her tone dismissive.

Her indifference irked Zita. Instead of the usual gossip and gore, a story about these kids and the impact Daniel's camp could make on a young life could be inspiring. But apparently murder and mayhem sold papers. Even if the murder occurred fifteen years ago.

"Will Beatrice and Floyd Torkel talk with me about Clive and the necklace?" Brandy's questions quickly returned to the murder.

The Torkels cooperate? Zita didn't picture that happening. She had trouble finding anything positive to say. "I wouldn't hazard a guess as to how they'll respond to your questions."

"Oh, by the way, I hired a local diver to go down in the lake with me tomorrow. We're going to inspect the fish crib and he'll take underwater pictures. Should give added impact to my article."

Zita found the idea of searching the crib where Clive's body had been all these years disgusting. She wondered if the police would allow someone at the crime scene. Obviously there wouldn't be any yellow crime tape surrounding the fish crib. "Are the police allowing divers?"

"When I spoke to the police, I asked permission. Not a

problem. They're finished with the site. They might have missed something."

"I'm sure they were thorough," Zita said, picturing the lake becoming a site of morbid interest for divers.

"Besides pictures, I'm renting a metal detector. With all the brush and weeds, there still might be something of interest down there."

Zita couldn't stop herself from pondering Brandy's words. What else could be down there? Her imagination caused vivid images, revolting images of gangsters using her lake as a body dump.

"Do you have a problem with my exploring a bit?"

Brandy's question jerked Zita back. Did she have a problem? "I can't prevent you from diving. You will hand over to the police anything you find that involves their investigation?"

"Of course."

The response came too quickly. Zita had trouble trusting this reporter. She would talk this over with Kimmy and then call Roger.

CHAPTER EIGHT

Thursday afternoon, Zita walked down to the pier. Brandy
and her diving partner were entering the lake. They wore black
wet suits with air tanks strapped to their backs. Zita had never
observed divers up close. All the equipment fascinated her—
masks, breathing regulators, weight belts, and fins. Brandy
carried the metal detector and her dive partner had the
underwater camera.

Once they were in the water and dove out of sight near the
fish crib, Zita climbed up the incline to the house. There wouldn't
be anything of interest until they resurfaced.

She stopped on the deck to enjoy the view, her gaze
skimming the water over the crib. Only a diver's flag bobbing on
the surface of the water for safety indicated the scuba divers
beneath the surface. Even contemplating exploring the area
where Clive's body had been all those years made her queasy.

Inhaling the pine-scented air, she wanted to pause and enjoy
this perfect spring afternoon. The ducks and loons had returned
and were nesting on the lake. The placid surface reflected the
evergreen trees along the shore. More bubbles disturbed the
water. She wondered if there would be one day this summer free

of chaos. Any pleasure she had received from the tranquil view evaporated.

Kimmy opened the patio door, motioning for Zita to come inside. "There's a customer on the phone. They want to place an order for a sign."

Zita walked into the kitchen and took the phone from Kimmy. "Hello, this is Zita Stillman. Yes, I did make that eight-foot tall stork to announce their baby's birth." She spotted a note on the counter. Only half listening to the caller, panic swept through her. She had trouble picking up the thread of conversation. "Yes, your order will be ready Memorial Day weekend." She returned the receiver to the base on the counter.

"When did Heather call?"

"Oh, Auntie, I'm sorry. I forgot." Kimmy stood up. "She called while you were having lunch with Zinnia."

"Did she say what she wanted?"

"No but she did sound upset," Kimmy said.

Uneasiness settled into the pit of Zita's stomach. Heather never called her. She wondered if this had anything to do with a health issue. The memory of their strange encounter at the clinic remained disturbingly clear. Her hand shook as she lifted the receiver and dialed. Heather answered on the second ring.

"Yes, Kimmy told me you called. Of course, I can be there in ten minutes." As Zita hung up the phone, she continued to tremble. Something must have happened. Something she couldn't share with her niece.

"Auntie what's wrong?"

"I'm not sure. She wants me to meet her at Torpy Park." Zita noticed movement in the water near the fish crib. "I need to leave now. Keep an eye on the divers for me. I have misgivings regarding Brandy. She might do anything to gain recognition by writing an exposé surrounding the murder."

Zita grabbed her purse and hurried to the garage. She sprinted from one worrisome event to the next. Heather's news must be unbearable for her daughter-in-law to call.

❀⋎　⋎❀

Zita arrived at the park, praying all the way. Frightening images permeated her thoughts. Would she be able to handle another devastating illness? Did Jim know? She doubted he did. Why else would Heather call her?

As she exited the car, her hands trembled. Glancing around, she scanned the park to locate Heather. Several mothers were on the playground with their children. An older couple sat at one of the picnic tables. She saw a man walking on the sand along the lake shore.

Heather's car was parked in the lot. She had to be here somewhere. Girding herself for whatever she might face, Zita climbed the steps to the pavilion. The shadowy interior of the open structure was damp and chilly. Slowly her eyes adjusted to the dim lighting.

A rustle of sound drew her attention to a far corner. Someone sat huddled against the wall. Zita hurried forward, softly calling Heather's name. Deep sobs were the only response.

Zita hurried to sit down next to her daughter-in-law on the hard cement bench. Heather turned her tear-streaked face toward Zita. Without a word, Zita opened her arms. With an agonizing wail of despair, Heather crumbled into Zita's embrace.

Zita's heart ached as she prayed for words of comfort and wisdom. Her fragile composure cracked. Could their family handle another calamity? Emotionally, she had nothing left to give.

Rubbing Heather's back gently, Zita found the courage to ask the question, "Honey, what's wrong?"

Heather hiccupped, her sobs subsiding. Pulling away from Zita, she wiped at her red, puffy eyes with a wadded-up tissue. After blowing her nose, she stared down at her lap. "What should I do? This can't wait any longer, I have to tell Jim." Her voice was barely above a whisper.

Doubts and fears assailed Zita. She reached over, covering

Heather's hands with her own. "You are my daughter. I love you." As she said the words, she knew they were true. "We're family. We can get through anything together."

Heather moved restlessly on the bench. Her lips were pressed tightly together as she clasped and unclasped her hands.

Icy fear twisted around Zita's heart. "Please, tell me."

Heather's cheeks turned a fiery scarlet. "I'm pregnant," she blurted out.

A soft gasp escaped Zita's lips, followed by shocked astonishment, and most of all relief. *Pregnant. A baby. A grandchild.* Joy bubbled up inside. How should she respond to this news? "I'm so relieved. When I saw you crying in the car that day at the clinic, I imagined all sorts of horrible things. Even cancer."

"Jim and I assumed we couldn't have children. Our careers kept us busy, and we never pursued medical options or opinions." Heather sounded as though she were thinking out loud. Her voice held a note of hysteria like a fragile thread frayed and ready to break. "But now... the worst time possible. We've lost everything and we're starting over. Jim doesn't need this extra burden."

A war of emotions battled through Zita. What had happened to this level-headed young woman who marched through life taking no prisoners? Heather seemed confused and out of control.

Zita sought words of encouragement. "Worst time? If nothing else, I've learned life happens. You have family here, you're not alone. My son will be—ecstatic. How far along are you? You saw a doctor? Is everything okay?"

Heather's eyes glazed over. "Twelve weeks. I saw the doctor the day you saw me in the clinic parking lot. I had what I assumed were ongoing flu symptoms. Not flu." She let out a long audible breath. "Morning sickness. Because of my age, he ordered an ultrasound today. I didn't want to tell Jim until after the test."

A wedge of fear sliced through Zita. What had the test revealed? Is that what caused Heather's emotional breakdown? Her fingers curled tightly into her palms. "Is the baby okay?"

Heather cried and laughed at the same time. Tears trickled

down her cheeks.

The odd reaction frightened Zita. *Is she hysterical?* "What were the results? How is the baby?" Her high-pitched voice sounded frantic in her ears.

Heather broke off mid-whimper. "Babies. We're having twins." She slumped back against the wall.

The shock of Heather's words left Zita too stunned to speak. *Twins!*

More tissues were added to the clump in Heather's hand. She mopped at the tears. "Jodie Chatwyn. Jim has her working at the hotel. I'm aware they were high school sweethearts." She sat up straight, shoulders back and stiff. Her jaw clenched. "Jim's probably sorry he married me. And now this. What am I going to do?"

Jodie showed up everywhere with Jim lately. Zita was increasingly uneasy over their relationship. But if her son had an ounce of his father in him, he would never be unfaithful to Heather. "No." Zita objected, finding her voice. "Jim loves you. Jodie is only an old friend going through a difficult time." Her conviction of that truth strengthened. She tucked an arm through Heather's. "This is wonderful, amazing news. Please, go home and invite your husband out to dinner. Someplace romantic. Tell him tonight."

"We can't afford to go out and waste money," Heather said, sounding dejected and disappointed.

A heaviness centered in Zita's chest. She ached for Heather. "You have to celebrate this magnificent news." She reached into her purse and removed her wallet. After removing all the bills, she handed them to Heather.

"I can't take that," Heather protested.

"Please, I want to. This is the most significant event of your life together. Make it memorable." Zita wanted to share in this celebration of life.

Hesitating briefly, Heather spoke indecisively, "I could wear a nice dress." She glanced down at her waist. "I might not be able to do that much longer."

"Exactly." Zita chuckled. "Twins, huh?"

"The doctor said they might be fraternal, a boy and a girl. It's too early to be certain. But the ultrasound was able to detect the possibility."

Once again Heather's news robbed Zita of the ability to speak. She couldn't hold back the tears of joy that slid down her cheeks. The wonderful news continued to multiply. "You'll have to call your parents. They will be so excited." The second the words left Zita's mouth, she wanted to snatch them back.

"I love Jim, but my parents disowned me when I married him. I'm sure you heard the Jonathon Stanbury story. They were angry when I didn't obey their wishes and marry the Stanbury Brokerage Firm."

"But grandchildren," Zita said. She couldn't imagine disowning a child. To erase them completely from your life.

Heather lifted one shoulder in a weak shrug. "If nothing else, Chrystal and Alastair Mackinnon can hold a grudge. I'm a disgrace. There's been no contact in ten years. After the first year of refusing to take my phone calls, I gave up." Once again she leaned into Zita, sobbing.

Zita shuddered inwardly at the pain Heather's parents had inflicted on their daughter. Ten wasted years. For her, life centered on her family and friends. And now, God had blessed her by enlarging that circle. Like a pebble dropped into the lake, her circle continued to expand outward.

Minutes passed. The wracking cries slowly subsided. Heather mopped at her eyes with a fresh tissue. "Zita, I owe you an apology. All these years, I've acted like a snob. You deserved better." A blush like a shadow rose in her cheeks.

"You don't need to apologize," Zita protested. These were words she never expected to hear. Her daughter-in-law had apparently grown and changed for the better over the past weeks.

"Yes, I do, "Heather continued. "I wanted to prove to my parents that Jim and I could climb the social ladder in Chicago."

She gave a rueful laugh. "Look where that got me." She clasped her hands tightly together in her lap. "Because of the way I've acted, I'm embarrassed to admit that I've fallen in love with Arbor Vale. I never acknowledged how unhappy Jim was in the city. Zita, he's so happy living here, working at the hotel, being around old friends and family. Every day I became more and more convinced of my selfishness."

Zita bubbled over with all these blessings being lavished upon her. She offered a silent prayer of thankfulness. Once again, she hugged Heather to her. "You need to go home and share this wonderful news with your husband."

"I want our children to grow up here. Arbor Vale produced my wonderful husband." She tucked the money Zita had given her into a pocket. "Thank you, Mom." Her eyes sparkled and her cheeks turned pink as she hurried away.

Mom. A warm glow spread through Zita. Her heart sang. She gave a sigh of contentment. Voices interrupted her delight. People were entering the pavilion. She wanted to remain hidden away in the corner, but the cool, dim interior was quickly losing its charm.

Someone spoke in a weak and tremulous whisper. Zita observed the new arrivals. A man pushing a wheelchair spoke calmly. "Suzanne, I'll only tell Jodie the truth if necessary."

Bewildered, Zita stood and stepped behind a pillar as Suzanne Chatwyn and Kenneth Hardgrave moved farther away. Were they discussing a secret? Something to do with Clive's death? She wasn't able to hear any further conversation. But memory of the murder stepped in, stealing her joy.

Determined to recapture the happiness of Heather's news, Zita decided to stop on the way home and buy two baby gifts. Identical baby gifts, one in blue and one in pink. She never expected to receive this blessing. Grandchildren. In the past half an hour, her whole life had turned upside down.

A few minutes later Zita parked in front of the Mommy Boutique. The window display held an array of colorful infant through toddler clothing. Excited by the prospect of buying something for her soon to be grandchildren, she hurried inside.

"Girlfriend, last place I expected to meet you," Zinnia said, emerging from behind a clothing rack.

Zita stiffened and then laughed to cover her annoyance. What excuse could she give for being here? Heather's condition needed to remain a secret for now.

"I'm here to by a gift for the baby shower they're having at church for Lisa Rayburn." Zinnia held up a footed flannel sleeper with lambs scattered across the fabric. "How about this?"

"That's adorable. Maybe I can find something to coordinate with that print." Relief skittered across Zita's nerves. Zinnia had provided her with the perfect excuse for being in the store.

"I love to buy baby gifts," Zinnia twittered. "I like what Charles Osgood said one time on the *CBS Morning News*: 'Babies are always more trouble than you thought—and more wonderful.'"

"They are wonderful," Zita agreed, unable to keep tears from forming. She quickly blinked them away. She didn't want to get all emotional in front of her friend and give away her secret joy.

"They had a crib blanket to match and some receiving blankets." Zinnia pointed toward the back of the store. "I wish I could stay and visit but I have to get back to the shop. Marta couldn't work today, she has a cold. So all the girls are doubling up to cover her clients."

Zita gave Zinnia a quick hug before walking toward the back of the store. Mannequins lined the aisles, wearing the latest maternity fashions. Things had certainly changed since she was pregnant with Jim. These dresses and pantsuits were feminine and stylish. She decided to get Heather a gift certificate for a special outfit.

After finding the coordinating lamb prints, Zita decided on the receiving blankets for Lisa's shower. Then she wandered the store, unable to decide what would be an appropriate gift for twin grandbabies. Heather had said she was at twelve weeks. That meant the babies would be born in November.

A far corner of the store exhibited a grouping of baby furniture. Zita suddenly realized Jim and Heather would need two of everything, from cribs to strollers.

"May I help you?"

Zita jerked. She hadn't heard the clerk walk up behind her.

"I didn't recognize you, Zita. Are you here buying a gift for Lisa?"

The excitement over this shopping trip faded. First Zinnia and now another friend from church. So much for spending time alone relishing the special grandbaby news. She held up the receiving blankets. "Yes. And I'm ready now." Not being able to buy a gift for the babies or Heather left her disappointed and frustrated.

"Would you like me to giftwrap the blankets?" the clerk asked.

"No, thank you," Zita replied. Right now all she wanted to do was escape from the store and further conversation.

"Lisa is registered here. And that is the pattern she chose for the nursery."

Warmth worked up Zita's neck and into her cheeks. "I should have asked. Thank you for telling me." Feeling foolish, she grasped the fact that Heather and Jim would also want to choose patterns and colors for their nursery. She had allowed her excitement to gallop out of control. When the time came, she would make sure to pick things they wanted.

After leaving the store with her purchase, Zita drove toward home. The memory of Heather using the word "Mom" returned, making her heart sing. She imagined Jim's reaction to Heather's news. Certainly her son would be jubilant. More importantly, the pregnancy would put an end to any uneasiness she had concerning Jim and Jodie.

When Zita arrived home, she hesitated before going into the

house. Kimmy would be sure to question her. She didn't want to upset her niece unnecessarily. But she didn't have the right to reveal news this personal. Not without permission.

When Kimmy met her in the breezeway, she hadn't reached a decision. "Auntie, I heard your car." Her eyes widened. "Heather's on the phone. She wants to talk with you." She turned back toward the kitchen then stopped. "Auntie, is something wrong? Is Heather sick?"

Zita calmed herself. "Let me talk to Heather first." She hoped to delay having to explain their meeting in the park to Kimmy as long as possible.

As she went to answer the phone, anxiety gnawed at Zita. She clenched the receiver in her hand. "Heather, is everything all right?"

"Yes, I'm sorry I put you in such a difficult position. You would never share my secret with anyone unless I gave you permission. Please feel free to tell Kimmy. I trust her to keep this confidential. But *please* don't tell Zinnia."

Relief rolled through Zita. Being able to tell Kimmy would make things easier. Besides a blessing shared doubled the joy. She put a hand to her mouth to stifle a giggle. "I promise to leave Zinnia to you. You deserve to see her reaction for yourself." Her cheerful mood lingered. "Thank you for allowing me to share this with Kimmy."

Heather laughed. "Yes, Zinnia. She is a delightful character. I'll enjoy being the one to tell her."

Kimmy stood a few feet away. Hearing her name being discussed, she leaned back against the wall, waiting. Her eyebrows were raised inquiringly.

"Thank you again, Mom. Jim agreed to go out to dinner tonight. He's a little puzzled. I can hardly wait. We have so much to plan for."

As soon as Zita hung up the phone, Kimmy asked, "What's going on? I've been worried since you left to meet Heather."

Zita touched Kimmy's arm. "We'd better sit down."

"Oh no! Bad news. What's wrong with Heather?" Kimmy slid onto a kitchen chair.

Zita joined her at the table. "Not bad news. Good news. Amazing news. This is confidential, but she gave me permission to tell you. Heather's pregnant."

"Wow! Has she told Jim? Is that why she's been acting so weird?" Kimmy leaned back against the chair. "Morning sickness? Right?"

"Exactly," Zita said. "Heather is going to tell Jim tonight. But there's more. She found out today that she's having twins." Tears of happiness filled Zita's eyes. Her joy intensified.

Kimmy's mouth dropped opened and she sputtered, "Twins? Are you kidding? No, I can tell you're not joking."

Wiping at the tears that trickled down her cheeks, Zita burst out laughing. "Can you handle the rest of the news?"

"I'm having trouble processing all of this. And there's more?"

"I feel the same way." Zita's smile widened into a grin. "Heather had an ultrasound today. The babies are fine and the doctor told Heather they're fraternal twins, a boy and a girl."

"Yikes! Awesome. This is wonderful news." Kimmy studied Zita before adding, "I can tell there's more. Good news?"

Zita couldn't prevent tears clouding her eyes or a giggle from escaping. "Honey, be prepared for another shock. Heather has fallen in love with Arbor Vale and wants to raise their children here."

"No way," Kimmy said, her intense astonishment evident in her voice. "Who replaced Heather with a body double?" She snapped her mouth shut, stunned.

"Heather shared so much, Kimmy. She's aware how happy Jim is, being back in Arbor Vale and managing the hotel."

"Kyla will have cousins to grow up with. I still can't believe Heather has done a complete turnaround. I guess she became distraught over losing everything, and being pregnant, she became withdrawn and frustrated. How far along is she?" Kimmy asked.

"Three months." Zita leaned forward and gripped Kimmy's hand. "She called me Mom."

CHAPTER NINE

After all the excitement over the babies, Zita had forgotten Brandy's peculiar dive over the fish crib until nearly supper time. She came in from the woodshop to find Kimmy and ask her about Brandy. Their guest's car wasn't parked in the driveway.

Kimmy and Kyla were sitting at the kitchen table. Kyla was playing more with her strained carrots than she was eating. There were smears of orange around her mouth and on her fingers. She opened her mouth like a little bird each time Kimmy brought up a spoonful.

"Someone is enjoying their supper," Zita said. Kyla's antics delighted her. Soon there would be two more babies in her life. She released a long sigh of contentment.

Kyla patted her hands on the tray, managing to splatter some orange goo in her mother's direction. Kimmy laughed and wiped Kyla's fingers with a wet cloth.

"I hate to interrupt the fun, but I wondered if anything came of Brandy's dive. Did she discover anything?" Zita sat down across from Kimmy.

Kimmy's lips puckered. The spoon stopped in midair until Kyla gave a demanding screech. Kimmy quickly slipped the spoon into Kyla's mouth. "Last one, honey." She scooped up a few Cheerios and placed them on the tray. "Finger food time."

"After the dive, Brandy acted a little weird. When she came into the breezeway, I went out and asked if she had found anything. She was excited but secretive. Denied discovering any evidence."

"What do you mean, 'secretive'?"

"When I questioned Brandy about the dive, she rushed downstairs to change without another word." Kimmy gave an impatient shrug. "It's hard to describe something you only sense."

"Even if Brandy did discover evidence, I doubt she would take it to the police. That woman is totally into her career," Zita said. "She's seeking a once-in-a-lifetime career-making story." Zita hesitated, wondering how to find out the truth from Brandy. "Did the man she dove with leave at the same time?"

"He came up from the lake and waited in the breezeway to retrieve the rest of Brandy's rented equipment." Kyla slapped the tray of her highchair with her chubby little hands. Kimmy placed a few more Cheerios on the tray. The baby squealed with delight, grabbing one.

Zita's memories of Jim at that age were precious. Time passed too quickly. Thoughts of her new grandbabies filled her with a warm glow.

"He commented on the clarity of the water and said the fish crib had deteriorated extensively. Over time the logs and brush have rotted and collapsed," Kimmy said, popping a few Cheerios into her own mouth. "He remarked that the lake must have a lot of oxygen in the water for that to happen. The only things holding the frame together were chains and cement blocks."

"Lorman chained cement blocks to the crib to make it sink. But did the diver find anything important?"

"He brought up a bag full of fishing lures. Must be a great place to snag your line and lose your bait," Kimmy said. "Some of the muskie lures were huge. How big are the fish in this lake?"

"Big." Zita stretched her arms out as far as they could reach.

"No way!"

"The largest one Lorman ever caught was over forty-six inches."

Lifting Kyla from the high chair, Kimmy grimaced. "I might muskie fish this summer, but I doubt I'll be swimming."

"When did Brandy leave?" Zita asked. "Her car is gone."

"She left immediately after returning the diving gear." Kimmy carried Kyla down the hall. "Somebody needs their diaper changed."

"Did Brandy say where she was going?" Zita called after her niece.

"No. Why?"

"Just curious." The foreboding she experienced earlier became a full-blown premonition that something dreadful was about to happen.

Zita awoke from a sound sleep. Had she heard something? Tense, she listened. Nothing. After a few minutes she roused herself and went to get a drink of water. Peering out the front window, she noted that Brandy's car still hadn't returned. Where could the young woman be at nearly three o'clock in the morning?

Again the uneasy feeling crept in. Zita's mothering instincts kicked into overdrive. She chastened herself for being overly protective. Brandy was an adult. If she chose to spend the night out... *None of my business.*

Once back in bed, she continued to listen for the sound of Brandy's car. Eventually sleep won.

The next morning, a bleary-eyed Zita wandered into the kitchen. Kimmy had already fed Kyla. The baby welcomed Zita with an excited screech and clapped her hands together.

Zita walked over and kissed Kyla's cheek. "How's my sweetie this morning? Have you learned to play patty-cake?"

"Brandy must have had an early appointment this morning," Kimmy commented. "Her car is gone. Do you think she'll want breakfast later?"

Zita didn't want to overreact and upset Kimmy. "Brandy didn't come home last night." She poured a cup of coffee and took a drink.

"What?' Kimmy stopped stirring the pan of scrambled eggs. "How do you know?"

"I got up around three for a glass of water. Her car wasn't in the driveway."

Turning off the stove, Kimmy opened the cabinet and removed two plates. "Should we be concerned?" She spooned the eggs onto the dishes and carried them to the table.

"I am." Zita sat down at the table, hugging her coffee cup. "Isn't there some rule about having to wait forty-eight hours before reporting a missing person?"

They heard a car door slam. "Maybe that's her now," Zita said, shoving back her chair and standing. By the time she opened the kitchen door, Roger had entered the breezeway.

"Good morning," he said, removing his cap. "I came by to talk with your guest. Is Brandy Gardell still staying with you?"

Zita didn't like the sound of this. Was she being sucked into yet another problem? "Yes, we were going to call you this morning. What's happened?"

Without answering Zita's question, Roger asked another. "Why were you going to call?"

Zita's nervousness over Brandy's absence heightened.

"Brandy didn't come home last night and we're worried," Kimmy said.

Roger sighed. "That's what I was afraid of. An officer discovered her vehicle parked overnight at Spider Lake beach. In her glove compartment, he found a receipt for your bed-and-breakfast. That's how he traced her back to you."

None of this made any sense to Zita. Her fears grew stronger than ever. "Why would Brandy have a reason to go to Spider Lake?"

"That would have been my next question," Roger said.

"Could she be…?" Kimmy paused, running her fingers across the tabletop.

Zita knew exactly what Kimmy meant. The possibility was too horrific to say aloud. Would they find Brandy alive? Had she drowned?

"The department is preparing to call out the dive team…in case," Roger said.

Zita flinched. Maybe they needed to explain to Roger the curious way Brandy behaved after the dive. She would never have gone to Spider Lake to swim, especially at night. Maybe to meet someone? If they found her body, it might mean foul play and another murder.

"With your permission, I'd like to examine her bedroom," Roger said. "There might be a clue to what's happened to her."

Zita led Roger downstairs.

"Did Brandy make or receive any phone calls?" Roger asked.

"Not from our phone. But she had a cell phone. I have her number."

"I'll get a warrant to contact her server to access her phone records," Roger said.

The bedroom was surprisingly neat. The bed hadn't been slept in. A notebook and laptop computer were on the desk.

"Brandy's a reporter for which newspaper?" Roger asked.

"For a tabloid called *The Tattler.*"

"Anything else you can tell me?"

"She's from Milwaukee. And then there was the dive yesterday."

"What dive?"

"Yesterday afternoon, Brandy dove over the crib with the owner of the local dive shop. The one on the highway. She even had an underwater camera and a metal detector."

The information bothered Roger. His jaw clenched.

Zita sensed she should have cleared this dive with Roger. "Brandy told us she had spoken with the police and had permission to inspect the crib."

"News to me," Roger said in an abrupt tone. "Impossible to keep people away from the site. We don't have the manpower."

"I wasn't here, but Kimmy spoke with Brandy afterward. She apparently acted suspicious, as though she might have found something."

"Great," Roger grumbled. "This gets better and better. Why don't people leave the investigating to the professionals? All we need is some nosy reporter confronting Clive's killer."

That had been one of the things that troubled Zita during the night. Hearing the words aloud stabbed her with guilt. She and Zinnia had gotten in trouble in the past, doing exactly that. Roger's words left her wondering if she could have done something to prevent... what? A drowning, a kidnapping, or another murder?

"I'll see if Kimmy has anything to add to our investigation." Roger glanced around the room. "And I'll need a warrant to access her computer and notebook also."

All the way up the stairs, Zita pondered this new development. Was it related to Clive's murder? After all these years, would it bring a new danger to her family?

Roger and Zita returned to the kitchen.

"Zita said you mentioned Brandy acted suspicious after the dive. Is there anything specific?" he asked Kimmy.

"Not really. Brandy insisted on immediately removing the film from the underwater camera. It wasn't digital. Her dive partner owned the camera and acted surprised by her demand." Kimmy placed a few small pieces of scrambled eggs on Kyla's tray.

"Maybe she left the film to be developed locally. There can't be many businesses that do that anymore," Zita commented. "Was there any sign of a struggle where you found her car?"

"Good catch on the film. I'll start calling around," Roger said. "No sign of a struggle. Hard to tell if the car was dumped there. No keys or purse. She might have gone off with someone willingly. But the dive team will be on site this morning."

This was all sickeningly familiar to Zita. Had she become trapped in another maze of evil?

Roger fidgeted. "I'm off-duty tonight, Kimmy. Would you like to go out for Friday fish fry?"

"I'll babysit Kyla." Zita jumped in.

Kimmy glowed with happiness. "I'd love to go for dinner."

He beamed at Kimmy. "Great. I'll pick you up around seven." He hurried out the door.

"Thanks for offering to care for Kyla. Roger and I hardly ever have an opportunity to spend time alone. I hope there aren't any burglaries or murder victims during our dinner date." Kimmy reached for her glass of orange juice.

Zita prayed Brandy would arrive safely and that this had all been a misunderstanding. In her heart, she was filled with doubts. The way things had been going in her life, Zita's misgivings only increased.

After clearing the table, Kimmy lifted Kyla from the high chair. "We haven't heard anything from Jim or Heather. I wonder how he reacted to the news."

At the mention of the pregnancy, Zita perked up. "I'm sure they have marvelous plans to share. The first since their lives fell apart in Chicago. I still can't believe I'm going to be a grandmother of twins." Tears flooded her eyes. "I wish Lorman could have lived to hold his grandchildren."

"I feel the same way. Kyle would have adored our daughter." Kimmy patted Zita's hand.

Zita wiped away the tears with her napkin. She needed to resist these depressing memories and move on. "I'm going to the hotel this morning. Daniel is expecting two new campers tonight for the weekend. I'll see if Jim needs any help getting rooms ready." Zita took a final drink of coffee. "At least nothing should go wrong with these little girls during their stay."

CHAPTER TEN

While driving to the hotel, Brandy's disappearance claimed Zita's attention. She had difficulty concentrating on the road.

When Zita arrived, Jim flung open the door. He grabbed her into a tight hug and then danced her around the lobby. The steps were a quirky concoction of a polka and tango. Breathless and laughing, they collapsed onto the loveseat. He could barely contain his joy.

"Mom, I'm so excited, I could explode. Twins!"

Zita patted his hand. "This is an amazing gift." She was thankful that these babies were having a positive effect on Jim and Heather's relationship. Footsteps thumped overhead. "Is Heather upstairs?"

"No, she insisted on going to work at the bookstore today. I wanted her to stay home and rest."

"Heather is healthy. The doctor doesn't have her on any restrictions. She'll enjoy being active before the babies arrive," Zita said. She remembered bringing Jim home from the hospital and how much time caring for one baby consumed. Twins would be overwhelming.

Again footsteps resonated from the second floor.

"Do you have guests registered?" Zita asked. "I came to help prepare rooms for the weekend. Especially for the girls staying here for Daniel's camp."

"Jodie came in to work today. She might need some help."

Zita wondered if Jodie's presence would continue to be a problem for Heather. Spending time working with Jodie might help her gauge the young woman's intent concerning Jim.

"Mom, when Jodie arrived, she was upset. You're good with people. Maybe you can find out what's up. Her mom might be worse."

Great. Why me? Zita hated being put in these situations. She had witnessed the times Jodie sought out her son and Heather's jealous reaction. Could Jodie's intentions toward Jim have been thwarted because of the pregnancy?

"Thanks, Mom. If you need me, I'll be downstairs doing laundry."

Zita wondered when she had agreed to confront Jodie's problems. Trudging slowly up the stairs, she dreaded an encounter with Clive's daughter.

Zita and Jodie nearly collided in the hallway. Zita steadied herself by gripping a doorframe. Jodie dropped an armload of bedding on the floor.

"Sorry. I wasn't paying attention," Jodie apologized. Her eyes were red and swollen from crying.

Zita's mothering and nurturing instincts kicked in. She wrapped her arms around Jodie, and the young woman leaned into Zita, sobbing.

"Honey, what's wrong?" *Please, please don't say Jim.*

"I moved Mom into the hospice house yesterday." Jodie pulled away from Zita, still sniffling. She pointed to an antique wooden bench. "Could we sit down? I need to talk with someone. My life is in chaos."

"Absolutely." Zita understood Jodie didn't need advice, but someone to listen.

They sat side by side on the bench. Staring at the floor, Jodie rested her arms on her knees. "I'm helpless and inadequate. I physically couldn't care for Mom alone." She started weeping.

"You shouldn't be working today," Zita said. "Go, be with her."

"Kenneth Hardgrave is there. They need time alone together. Ken has always been devoted to Mom, but last night she told me that he's my father." Jodie stiffened and leaned back against the wall.

This news jolted Zita. But she sympathized with Jodie. Only recently she had found out the truth regarding her birthparents. Even now she had trouble grasping the reality of the mother who had abandoned her. "Your father? I don't understand."

"I wish I did," Jodie mumbled. "Talk about your deathbed confession. If Clive had found out that little secret, we'd all be dead."

Zita's heart thumped loudly. What if Clive had found out the truth about Suzanne's affair and the fact that Ken was Jodie's father? Had there been a confrontation between Clive and Ken?

"Ken has been there for Mom and me." Jodie peeked at Zita out of the corner of her eye. "Are you shocked?"

Awkwardly, Zita cleared her throat. The infidelity didn't shock her as much as the possibility that the affair might have caused Clive's murder.

"I didn't believe my life could get any worse. Now pandemonium has landed full force." Jodie wiped at the tears on her cheeks. "And his name is Trace."

"Who's Trace?" Zita hesitated. This was becoming complicated.

"Trace is my ex. He showed up last night and is pushing for us to get back together." A single tear trickled down her cheek. "Mom only has a few days, maybe a week left. Emotionally, I can't deal with Trace now."

"I wasn't scheduled to work today. I came here to hide from everyone. A quiet place to keep busy." Jodie wiped the tears from her eyes with her hands. "Thank you. I can't talk to Mom now.

You were always kind to me when Jim and I were dating. I want you to know how much that meant to me."

Jodie stood up abruptly. "I need to get these sheets down to the laundry." She gave Zita a quick hug then hurried down the stairs.

Zita remained sitting in stunned silence, processing all this new information. She assumed that Jodie was relieved that Clive wasn't her father. Clive was an evil, vindictive man. But if he had learned the truth that Jodie wasn't his daughter, the news may have played a part in his murder. Zita pondered whether to share this development with Roger. She wouldn't break a confidence unless absolutely necessary. At any rate, that decision would have to wait. Rooms needed to be cleaned.

Jim came up the stairs carrying an armload of clean towels and looking perplexed. "What happened with Jodie? She left, saying it was time to confront things head-on."

"I have no idea. She's in turmoil. Her mom was moved to the hospice house yesterday." Zita wondered which person Jodie planned to deal with, her mom, Kenneth Hardgrave, or her ex-husband.

"Poor Jodie." Jim's tone remained serious. "She's never had it easy." He scanned the room. "I'll stay and help finish the cleaning." He brightened and grinned. "We can discuss plans for the babies."

"Yes, the babies." Something wonderful to put Clive out of her mind. And her possible future visit with Roger.

Zita's thoughts filtered back to Brandy and her concern over their missing guest. "Our bed-and-breakfast guest has disappeared," she blurted out. She had gotten so caught up with Jodie's problems that she had forgotten to tell Jim.

"Disappeared!" Jim dropped the clean towels on the bed. "What do you mean, disappeared? Did she skip out without paying?"

"Yoo-hoo!" Zinnia shouted from the lobby. "Are you upstairs cousin?"

"Come on up!" Zita called. "Don't mention Brandy, we'll talk later," she said in hushed tones.

Trotting into the room, Zinnia flung her arms around Jim. "Heather stopped by on the way to the bookstore. How exciting, twins. I still can't believe it." She shook her finger at Zita. "You've had yourself a busy day. Why didn't you call and tell me all that's been happening? Stuff sure does whiz around in your life."

"Whiz around?" It was as though she was trapped in a hornets' nest. And Zita wanted it to end. "This was Heather and Jim's news to share."

"I want the inside info on your missing house guest, that reporter Brandy Gardell," Zinnia huffed. "If something has happened to her, I won't get my name in *The Tattler*. After I told everyone my picture and interview would be featured because of Clive's murder."

"Mom, what's happened?" Jim asked.

Zita cringed. If the beauty shop knew, the whole town would be buzzing because another incident involved her. Murder and mayhem continued to stalk her.

"The police dive team is out on Spider Lake, searching for her body." Zinnia was on a roll. "Word is, Brandy found something during her dive to investigate the fish crib. Something that's connected to Clive's murderer." She broke off to catch her breath, peering at Zita. "Do you and Kimmy have any idea what she found? Have you told Roger?"

"Mom?" Jim hadn't moved since Zinnia's outburst.

Slumping onto the nearest chair, Zita held up her hands to ward off any further questions. Why did people assume she had inside information about every burglary or murder? "Please make sure everyone understands that Kimmy and I are not involved in Brandy's disappearance. And she did not discuss any discovery made during her dive."

Footsteps sounded on the staircase. Zinnia zipped out to see who had arrived. "It's Roger. Now maybe I'll get some answers. Did you find her body? Was she murdered?"

111

Zita remained absolutely motionless. This was getting out of control. *Enough.*

Whenever Roger dealt with Zinnia, he'd go into panic mode. Today was no exception. He held up his hands to ward off her attack of questions. "Kimmy said you were here, Zita." He scowled at Zinnia for an instant. "Could we step into one of the rooms? I need to speak with you privately."

Zinnia made a huffy sound. "I guess I'll go back to the shop." With a glare in Roger's direction, she turned to leave. "I *will* call you later, girlfriend."

Zita knew what that meant. Zinnia would be furious if she didn't disclose whatever news Roger had to share.

Roger and Zita walked into the closest room and he shut the door. "I wanted you to hear this first, and I expect you to respect the confidentiality of this information. Brandy's body has not been found in Spider Lake. And she didn't take film into any local developers. Her diving partner agreed that she may have discovered something by the crib. She ended the dive abruptly and insisted on removing the film from his camera."

Zita wondered if this was the proper time to disclose Jodie's revelation. She decided against revealing that bit of news.

"Is there anything more you can tell me about Brandy, Zita?" Roger asked as they walked downstairs.

She shook her head.

Reaching the lobby, they discovered Zinnia waiting. "Any rumors at the beauty shop that might help the police, Zinnia?" Roger asked.

"Jodie's mom was moved to the hospice house," Zinnia said, listing things on her fingers. "Betty ran a stop sign and got a ticket. Third time this month. Might lose her license. Getting too old to drive. Jodie's ex-husband is in town, attempting to win her back. I doubt that will happen."

Zita couldn't keep up, wondering if they heard things at the beauty shop before they even happened. She waited to hear what came next. Had they heard the news about Jodie's parentage?

"Sarah's dog, Dabney, ran away. Wound up at the dog pound. She had to bail him out." Zinnia continued with her eruption. "Torkel's Treasures is locked up tight. That never happens, especially on a weekday. Beatrice might miss out on a dollar. Oh, and best of all, Heather and Jim are expecting twins." She ended with a grin.

Astonished by the news, Roger jerked around toward Jim for confirmation.

"Yes, twins," Jim said. "This will be quite an adjustment. But we're excited and thankful."

A few minutes later Roger and Zinnia left. Zita wondered, since the dive team hadn't recovered a body, if there was hope that Brandy might turn up alive.

Zita still struggled with revealing the truth of Jodie's parentage to Roger. She finally convinced herself she could wait on that decision. And there certainly was no need to tell Jim of this new development.

Working with Jim, she cleaned and organized the remaining rooms. As she smoothed the last quilt in place, excited, chattering voices echoed up from the lobby. Apparently the two young girls for Daniel's camp had arrived. Zita wondered where Daniel was. He should have been here to greet them.

Zita followed Jim down the staircase to welcome the new arrivals, and was surprised to see not two, but three little girls. They were eight or nine years old. Two of the girls were identical twins, dark hair and eyes, with giggles and grins.

"I'm, Jenna," the chaperone announced. "These two pranksters are Aubrey and Alexis. Good luck telling them apart."

"Aubrey's taller and the tip of her nose turns up," the third girl interrupted.

"Does not," Aubrey protested, pushing on the tip of her nose.

"My sister is not taller than me," Alexis objected.

"Girls!" Jenna intervened. "No arguing this weekend."

Zita noted that the observation was accurate. Aubrey was a tad taller than her sister, and her nose did turn up ever so slightly. The third girl drew Zita's attention. The poor skinny little thing was a study in "sullen."

"Our third camper this weekend is Deirdre," Jenna announced.

Deirdre avoided eye contact. She was small and thin for her age. Her blond hair needed a good washing and brushing, her clothing was tattered and dirty.

Aubrey whispered something to Alexis, peering at Deirdre. Both girls snickered.

"That's enough," Jenna warned.

Deirdre's cheeks burned scarlet and her hands clenched into fists. Zita's heart ached for the obviously neglected little girl. "I'm Zita and this is my son, Jim. I'll show you to your room. And then I'll tell Daniel you've arrived." She hoped getting the group settled would defuse Deirdre's anger and embarrassment.

When Zita returned to the lobby, Daniel and Jim were deep in conversation by the reception desk.

"Jenna is a competent child therapist," Daniel said. "That's why she offered to chaperone the girls this weekend."

Daniels's words shouted, "problem," something Zita was ill-equipped to handle. Jim's worried frown only intensified her uneasiness.

Daniel motioned for Zita to join them at the desk. "I was filling Jim in on the situation. Jenna is Deirdre's case worker. The child has been removed from the family she was living with. Social Services are making other placement arrangements effective early next week. Jenna has a relationship with Deirdre and offered to care for her this weekend."

Sorrow for Deirdre weighed heavily on Zita. "What can I do to help?"

"She came with only the clothes she's wearing. Could you get some things in her size?" Daniel asked. "I'm sorry I didn't have time to discuss this with you and Jim. I wasn't called until an hour ago. They wanted her in a safe place for a few days, and I couldn't refuse."

Zita regarded her son seated across the desk from her and saw the sorrow etched in his expression. "Jim? Is this going to be okay with you and Heather?"

"Of course, Mom. But I'll need to explain this to Heather," Jim said.

"There is safety and confidentiality involved," Daniel explained. "The police have been informed. But this can't be discussed beyond the two of you and Heather."

"I'll go to Wal-Mart," Zita said. "Everything I buy will be washed. I don't want the twins to notice all new clothes and make comments to Deirdre. Should probably buy a small duffel bag too."

"Good idea, Mom," Jim said. "While you're gone, Daniel can help me put together a snack for the girls."

Reaching the door, Zita paused. "If there's any news of Brandy, call me."

"Has something happened to your bed-and-breakfast guest?" Daniel asked.

"She's missing," Zita said. Saying the words caused a fresh wave of fear to assail her. Was Brandy's disappearance connected to Clive's murder? Had she found a clue by the fish crib and confronted the killer alone?

Zita needed to concentrate on Deirdre. In the midst of all the turbulence in her life, she now had willingly added a tragic little waif of a girl. A neglected child, who was frightened and alone among strangers.

❀❳ ❳❀

By the time Zita finished shopping and then washing, drying, and packing Deirdre's clothing in the duffel bag, it was past her suppertime. She had almost reached her car when Zinnia raced across the street.

"Hold up cousin!" Zinnia called. Huffing and puffing, she leaned against the car.

Zita waited, wondering what gossip had her friend in a tizzy.

"Suzanne Chatwyn died," Zinnia said. "Everyone is speculating whether the truth of Clive's murder died with her. Could she have made a deathbed confession to killing her husband? If she took a secret like that to her grave, your family might remain under suspicion."

Jodie remained foremost in Zita's mind. The poor girl had lost her mother. Add together Clive's murder, news of Kenneth Hardgrave being her birthfather, and Trace, an ex-husband. Emotional chaos. "Is there anything we can do to help Jodie?"

"I'll call as soon as I hear anything," Zinnia said. "I left Lillian under the dryer. Have to run." She scooted back across the street.

Zita agonized over what she should do. Should she go back to the hotel and tell Jim the news and inform Roger of Jodie's parentage issue? Had she forgotten anything that might help the police find Brandy?

Zinnia's words haunted her. Could Suzanne have confessed to the murder? The possibility was shocking. Suzanne would have needed help to murder Clive and dump his body in the fish crib. Jodie or Kenneth could have been her accomplice.

Tiredness swept over Zita. Time to go home and rest. But the questions continued to buffet her. There would be no peaceful sleep tonight.

CHAPTER ELEVEN

Saturday morning, Zita stayed in her woodworking shop until lunchtime. The past week had held too many distractions. Orders were due to be picked up this afternoon. After putting the final touches of paint on several silhouettes and staining two shelves, she turned out the lights.

Kimmy had run interference by waiting on walk-in customers and answering the phone. There was still no word concerning Brandy.

When Zita entered the kitchen, Kimmy handed her a list of messages. Several were customer orders. Zinnia had called with Suzanne's funeral information.

Once again the phone rang. This time Zita answered. Jim's panicked voice greeted her. "Mom, I need you."

Alarmed, Zita feared something had happened to Heather and the twins. "The babies?"

Jim had already broken the connection.

"Something wrong at the hotel!" Zita shouted to Kimmy as she raced for the door.

Within minutes Zita arrived at the hotel to hear raised voices coming from Jim and Heather's apartment. She hesitated.

SIN LIETH AT THE DOOR

"Jonathan Stanbury," Heather said. "I had heard that tidbit of gossip." Her contemptuous tone made Zita cringe.

Jonathan Stanbury. Where she had heard that name?

"No contact for ten years and now you have the nerve to show up." Heather gave a bitter laugh.

Zita wilted with relief, realizing this emergency didn't involve the babies. But then she remembered Jonathon was the man Heather's parents had wanted her to marry. They disowned her when she married Jim. Zita's temper flared. Jim called because Heather's parents had arrived unannounced and he needed her help. But help to do what? Defuse the situation?

"Hello!" she called.

Jim stepped into the apartment doorway, his mouth tight with strain. "Hi, Mom, come on back, Heather's parents stopped by for a visit." His voice was deceptively calm.

Making a desperate attempt to smile, Zita walked across the lobby. Every step raised her level of anxiety. She wondered what Jim expected her to do.

Grim staring expressions met Zita. The sixty-something couple standing in the kitchen were overdressed for a weekend in Arbor Vale. They were tan and fit, dripping with class.

"Chrystal and Alastair MacKinnon, I'd like you to meet my mom, Zita." Jim's tone was courteous, but Zita caught the bitter edge in his voice.

Zita held out her hand to Alastair. He gave a firm handshake but remained tight-lipped. When Zita held out her hand to Chrystal, she only nodded. Rebuffed, Zita dropped her hand to her side.

So that's how it's going to be. Zita took a step back, striving to ignore Chrystal's rude behavior. Her attention centered on Heather. "How are you feeling today, sweetie?"

Heather's eyes widened and she gave a slight shake of her head. "I'm fine, Mom."

Zita caught the message not to mention Heather's pregnancy. But she also noted Chrystal's scowl when Heather referred to her as mom.

"You have quite a quaint little hotel here," Chrystal said. Her sarcastic tone contradicted her words.

Zita didn't play these games. "Thank you. I inherited the property from my aunt. I was thankful when Jim and Heather offered to manage it for me."

"I'm sure you were." Chrystal dismissed Zita and Jim, turning to Heather. "Your father has made a generous offer for you and your husband to return with us to New York."

When Chrystal refused to use Jim's name, Zita's heart sank. The word "husband" sounded like an insult. She bit her lip to prevent words she'd regret from popping out.

"The starting salary is adequate for an upscale home," Chrystal sneered, glancing around the kitchen. "And darling, you wouldn't have to work."

"You're only here because Jonathan's in jail. Yes, we do get national news here in little old Arbor Vale. He and his father have been convicted of insider trading. Goes to show how great your choices for my life have been."

"No need to take that tone with your mother," Alastair said. "That's all in the past. Forgotten. We're here to discuss your future."

"Well, you needn't have bothered. And I haven't forgotten. My future is here. When we had nowhere else to go, Zita took us in. I behaved horribly, but she loved me any way."

"You can't be serious," Chrystal said. "You weren't bred for this kind of life."

Heather gave a bitter laugh. "You make me sound like a racehorse. What kind of life did you breed me for? Oh, that's right; I could be living in disgrace with the Stanbury name."

Chrystal had the decency to blush.

Alastair cleared his throat. "Unfortunate circumstances. But as long as we're here, your mother and I would like you to consider our offer."

Heather turned her back to her parents with hands clenched

at her side. "Ten years," she mumbled.

Placing a tentative hand on her husband's arm, Chrystal said, "We need to find a decent place to stay tonight." With a final inspection of the kitchen, she gave a sniff of disdain.

Zita's hands curled into fists. Fortunately, Jim intervened and prevented her from expressing her contempt for the MacKinnons. "It's unfortunate our hotel doesn't have a vacancy this weekend," he said. He remained polite, but Zita saw the flash of contempt in his eyes. "Might be difficult to find a room without a reservation." He took Zita's arm. "I need to talk with you privately."

They'd barely reached the lobby when Jim leaned in and whispered, "Get them out of here, Mom. Heather doesn't need this kind of stress."

"What do you want me to do?"

He rubbed the back of his neck. "This is a lot to ask, but with Brandy missing, could they stay at the bed-and-breakfast?"

Zita flinched and her mouth dropped open. Her son had to be joking. Those snooty, rude people in her home?

Once again raised voices echoed out from the apartment.

Zita realized Jim and Heather were depending on her to handle the MacKinnons. She probably was better equipped to cope with the situation. Striding into the kitchen, she interrupted the exchange. "My niece and I have a bed-and-breakfast in our home. We'd enjoy having you stay with us." She almost choked on the word "enjoy."

Chrystal frowned at her husband. "I suppose if we have no other options."

Zita saw Heather's wide-eyed surprise. "Don't worry, sweetie." Kimmy and she had entertained far worse guests, including a murderer.

Zita suggested several of the local restaurants to Chrystal and Alastair for lunch. That would give her time to prepare the downstairs bedroom for them. When she left the hotel, Jim and Heather were both calmer. For now a crisis had been averted.

❋⤜ ⤛❋

When Zita rushed into the house, Kimmy asked, "Auntie, you frightened me. Are Jim and Heather okay?"

"Heather and the babies are fine," Zita reassured her. "But we have a bit of a complication."

"That sounds serious. What's happened?"

Zita frantically collected cleaning supplies. "Heather parents arrived, and they're staying with us."

"What if Brandy returns?" Kimmy went to the linen closet and grabbed some clean bedding and towels.

The mention of Brandy made Zita flinch. "This situation between Heather and her parents is beyond stressful. I had to get them out of the hotel. While they're staying with us, don't mention the babies. Heather doesn't want to tell them, at least not yet."

"Kyla's asleep. I'll take the baby monitor with me in case she wakes up. Working together, we should have things ready in less than an hour. What should we do with Brandy's things?"

"We'll pack her suitcases and put them in the garage. If she returns we'll give her the guest bedroom upstairs," Zita said.

"Brandy isn't coming back is she?" Kimmy said.

Zita couldn't bring herself to say what she dreaded, that Brandy was dead. If Brandy had discovered something in the fish crib, it meant Clive's murderer might have struck again.

They worked together carefully folding Brandy's clothes and then carried her suitcases up to the garage. After changing the bedding and towels, Zita dusted and vacuumed. Kimmy was busy cleaning the bathroom. As they climbed the stairs the doorbell sounded.

Zita gave a weary sigh. "Finished in time."

"I'll leave you to handle Heather's parents," Kimmy said, hurrying away into the house.

Zita opened the door to find Jodie Chatwyn instead of

Chrystal and Alastair. Jodie flung herself into Zita's arms, sobbing.

Zita held Jodie, rubbing her back. "I heard your mother died. I'm so sorry. Is there anything I can do?"

Jodie pulled away, wiping at her eyes.

Zita gasped when she saw Jodie's face. She had a black eye and a puffy split lip. "Jodie what happened? Should I call a doctor?"

"No doctor. I don't want this reported to the police. Trace would come after me harder next time. There's always a next time," Jodie said.

Shaken, Zita took the young woman by the arm and helped her into the kitchen.

"I'll get the ice pack from the freezer," Kimmy offered.

The three women went into the living room and settled Jodie in the recliner with the ice pack on her eye. Zita covered her with an afghan, fearful that Jodie might be going into shock.

Jodie's lips trembled. "Trace did this. I knew better than to let him back in my life. I believed he might have changed. He could talk a good game to get what he wanted."

Zita turned to Kimmy and whispered, "Call Roger, and make sure the door is locked. Better keep the shotgun handy."

With a quick nod, Kimmy left the room.

"Can you tell me what happened?" Zita asked.

"Trace apologized for everything that happened in our marriage. He claimed to have a good job and completed rehab for his drug and alcohol abuse. Not to mention his other abusive traits." Jodie gingerly touched her lip.

Zita noticed more bruises on Jodie's upper arms, and her shock turned to fury. "Why would he do this?"

"Trace learned of Mom's terminal illness. He had planned this visit even before she died. At first he was caring and comforting, but when I refused to sell the house and move back to the city with him, this happened. He doesn't love me. He just wants to get his hands on anything I might have inherited." A tear trickled down her cheek.

"You're safe here. We need to report this to the police and get a restraining order," Zita said.

"I'm sorry to drag you into my mess. When I managed to get away from Trace, I had nowhere else to go. If Ken finds out, I'm afraid he'll kill Trace. He's been very protective of Mom and me. I should have realized he was my father." Jodie moved the ice pack from her eye to her lip. She leaned back and closed both eyes.

"I'm thankful Kimmy and I are here to help."

The doorbell sounded again, jolting Zita. She saw Kimmy hurry toward the breezeway, twelve-gauge shot gun in hand.

An inappropriate grin twitched at the corners of Zita's mouth. If that was Heather's parents arriving, she imagined how they would feel being met at the door by her shotgun-brandishing niece.

When Zita heard Roger's voice, relief spurted through her. The cavalry had arrived. She glanced toward Jodie. The poor girl had fallen asleep. Zita went over and gently touched her arm. She jerked and opened her eyes wide with fear.

"I'm sorry, I didn't mean to startle you," Zita said. "Officer Roger Brooks is here. He'll be able to keep Trace from hurting you again."

Jodie sat up straighter, removing the ice pack from her lip. Zita noticed the swelling had gone down a bit.

"Jodie, I'm Roger," he said, entering the room. "Kimmy explained what happened to you. Are you willing to file charges against your ex-husband? Assault will violate his parole and put him back in prison."

"Prison?" Jodie asked.

"You didn't know?" Roger said. "Trace was released on parole recently. He was in prison for a drug-related crime."

Jodie shrank back into the chair. "Yes, I'll file charges. Thank you."

Once again the doorbell sounded.

"That must be Chrystal and Alastair," Zita said. "I'll get them settled downstairs." As she turned the deadbolt, the door was shoved violently open, knocking her against the wall. A very angry, very drunk young man staggered into the breezeway, wielding a hunting knife.

"Where's my wife?" he bellowed.

Zita hugged the wall, too terrified to move.

He took a step toward her, waving the knife. "I asked you where my wife is."

The smell of alcohol choked Zita. Her stomach roiled.

Movement in the doorway to the kitchen caught her eye.

Roger had his weapon drawn. "Trace, put down the knife," he ordered.

A sneer twisted Trace's lips. Raising his arms and shifting his weight, he snaked around toward Roger. In the same instant, Trace threw the knife and Roger fired.

A scream caught in Zita's throat as Trace hit the floor with a thud. The knife struck the wall next to Roger's head. Staring down at Trace, he called for backup and an ambulance.

Trembling and woozy, Zita gripped the door for support. She could hear Kyla crying. The gunshot must have frightened her. Now there were sirens in a distance.

Someone knocked on the door. Zita peeked around the edge of the doorframe and started to giggle. *I'm hysterical.* Of course, Heather's parents chose this moment to arrive. She opened the storm door, giggling harder. *They'll assume I'm insane, but I can't stop.*

"We're in a bit of a mess," Zita said, with tears running down her cheeks. "Chrystal and Alastair MacKinnon, I'd like you to meet Officer Roger Brooks. And Trace is the guy bleeding on my floor." She bit down hard on her lip to keep from laughing. "Sorry, I'm hysterical. Can you tell?"

The couple, eyes wide, started backing away from the door. Two squad cars and an ambulance flew into the driveway, blocking their escape.

Zita couldn't gain control of the situation. "Please, come

inside. I'll take you downstairs to the bedroom where you'll be out of the line of fire, I mean out of the way."

Their stunned expressions balanced between appalled and horrified, the MacKinnons followed Zita.

"Are you okay, Zita?" Roger asked, never taking his eyes off Trace.

With hands still shaking, Zita touched the growing lump on the back of her head and winced. "I'll live."

When the paramedics and officers rushed in the door, Zita continued down the stairs without another word.

"We won't be staying here!" Chrystal shrieked.

Another giggle threatened. Zita pinched herself hard on the arm to stifle it. "I understand. I'll come for you when it's safe to leave." Unable to tolerate another minute with the screeching Chrystal, Zita turned, retracing her steps. Jodie or Kimmy might need her.

Zita longed to avoid the chaos in her breezeway, but she had no choice. When she reached the top of the stairs, Trace's body was already strapped to a gurney. She was relieved when they wheeled him out the door, accompanied by the EMTs and a police officer. One crisis handled. She averted her eyes from the bloodstain on her carpet.

While Roger was taking notes and talking with Jodie, another officer took pictures of Jodie's injuries and the knife still stuck in the wall. Eyes wide, Kimmy stood in the kitchen, holding Kyla on her hip.

As the wail of the ambulance siren faded, the storm door flew open and Kenneth Hardgrave charged in. "Jodie!" he yelled frantically. Ignoring everyone in the room, he rushed to his daughter, wrapping his arms tightly around her. Pulling back, he examined her face. His jaw tightened. "Trace? Do you need a doctor?"

Jodie laid a restraining hand on his arm. "I'm fine. It's over, Ken." She pointed to the knife sticking out of the wall. "Trace tried to kill Officer Brooks, but the officer shot him. He's dead."

She leaned into her father, resting against his chest.

"Can I take Jodie home?" Ken asked Roger. "She needs to rest. Her mother's funeral is on Monday."

"Yes, I've finished with her statement for now," Roger answered. "Go home. Get some rest. If I have any more questions, I'll call you next week."

Jodie gripped Zita's hand on the way to the door. "Thank you for your help, Zita, I'm sorry I brought this mess to your house."

Zita smiled gently. "It's over. Take care, sweetie. I'll be at the funeral on Monday."

The remaining police officer, camera in hand, followed them out.

Kimmy, still holding Kyla, wrapped her free arm around Roger and kissed him. "I was so frightened. You could have been killed."

Roger clasped his arms protectively around Kimmy, cradling the baby between them. He gazed down into her eyes and then gently kissed her lips.

Zita stepped away to give them privacy.

The MacKinnons were working their way quietly up the stairs, furtively glancing around. They were apparently making their escape.

"We're leaving now," Chrystal said, moving hastily toward the door. Alastair trailed in her wake.

Unfortunately, their getaway was blocked by Zinnia bouncing through the door. Leave it to Zinnia to arrive all atwitter to find out the latest gossip. "Oh my, what's happened? I heard all sorts of reports on my police scanner."

The madness continued to unfold. It was like viewing a train wreck and being unable to prevent the disaster. Roger and Kimmy stepped apart. With gloves on, Roger pulled the knife from the wall, sliding the blade into a bag.

"Someone threw a knife?" Zinnia shrieked. "Is that blood on the floor? I heard shots had been fired."

The MacKinnons inched their way around Zinnia.

"Who are you?" Zinnia asked. Taking a step back, she blocked their path.

Hysteria threatened Zita's control. *I can't start laughing again.* "Chrystal and Alastair Mackinnon, I like you to meet my cousin, Zinnia Winwood."

"We're leaving," Chrystal said, attempting to push Zinnia aside.

Zinnia stiffened. "Emerson said, 'Life is not so short but that there is time for courtesy.'" She turned to Zita. "Who are these rude people and why are they in your home? Did they cause this mess?"

Zita heard a giggle from Kimmy. *No help there.* "These are Heather's parents. They were going to stay with us but…"

Zinnia interrupted, gushing, "Oh, you must be so excited,"

Would Zinnia blab the baby news? Zita screamed, "No!"

The MacKinnons and Zinnia glared at Zita as if she were insane.

"No, what?" Zinnia huffed. "I meant the twins."

Zita threw up her hands in despair. Why did she even try to contain Zinnia?

"Twins?" Chrystal said. "There must be something in the water in this town. You're all crazy." She shoved Zinnia roughly aside and thundered out the door.

Befuddled, Alastair followed, staring straight ahead.

Zita released a breath. The secret of her grandchildren was safe.

"What's up with them?" Zinnia asked, peering out the door.

"Heather hasn't told them she's pregnant. And they walked into the ongoing insanity in my life." Wearily, Zita rubbed her eyes. "I doubt if they'll ever come back to Arbor Vale."

"From what I've learned of the MacKinnons, that isn't a loss," Kimmy commented.

"Forget those people," Zinnia said. "Tell me all the details of what happened here."

"Jodie came here to hide after her ex-husband, Trace, hit her,"

Zita explained. "Fortunately, Roger got here before Trace showed up drunk with a knife. He threw the knife at Roger and Roger shot him."

"Wow! Girl, your life gets more dangerously exciting all the time." Zinnia quickly scanned the breezeway. "Where are Trace and Jodie now?"

"Trace is dead." Zita said. "And Jodie's father took her home."

"Jodie's father?" Roger and Zinnia said.

Oops, that's a secret. "Suzanne Chatwyn told Jodie the truth about her birthfather, and it isn't Clive," Zita stammered. "Kenneth Hardgrave is Jodie's natural father."

"And you didn't tell me this because…" Roger said.

"The secret wasn't mine to share," Zita said.

"Didn't you realize that information might have been a motive for Clive's murder?" Roger wrote something in his notebook. "From what I've heard, Clive would have gone after Hardgrave and Suzanne. Might be a case of self-defense. I will be talking with Jodie and Hardgrave after the funeral."

Frustration filled Zita. Why had she let that information slip? Between Suzanne's death and Trace's abuse, Jodie didn't need to be interrogated by the police. Zita had forgotten Zinnia was standing there, absorbing all this juicy gossip. "Zinnia, this information concerning Kenneth Hardgrave and Jodie is confidential, and you will not mention it to anyone."

"Fine," Zinnia huffed. She stared down at the blood pool on the floor. "With everything else that's happened, parentage doesn't even make the top ten in the latest town gossip."

Roger cleared his throat. "I will have to speak with Jodie and Hardgrave, Zita. But I'll wait until after the funeral." He leaned in and kissed Kimmy's cheek. "I have to go back to the station and start filling out paperwork. A mountain of paperwork. Anytime a weapon is discharged there is a complete investigation. Was deadly force necessary?"

"No doubt at all," Zita said. "I'm a witness." She wanted to putty up the mark in the wall as soon as possible. Realizing what might have happened made the lump on her head throb.

"You don't look so good, girlfriend," Zinnia said. "Were you hurt?"

"Trace shoved me back against the wall. Raised a bump on the back of my head." Zita touched the swollen area and winced.

"You'd better get some ice on that," Zinnia said. "I need to scurry back to the shop. The girls will be waiting to hear the latest Zita adventure. You're becoming quite famous."

Zita grimaced. She didn't need that type of fame. "Please don't mention anything concerning Kenneth Hardgrave or the twins. I'm sure the news of Jodie's parentage may be common knowledge soon enough."

Zinnia lifted her right hand. "Scouts honor."

"Get some rest," Roger said as he escorted Zinnia out the door.

Rest. But that delightful plan was interrupted by the phone ringing. Zita hurried to answer it.

"Mom, what did you do to Chrystal and Alastair?" Jim shouted.

CHAPTER TWELVE

Zita pulled a chair out from the kitchen table and collapsed onto it. The MacKinnons had wasted no time in reporting to their daughter.

"Chrystal came back to the hotel petrified." Jim continued his rant. "She's been shrieking that a man had been shot and was bleeding all over the carpet and there was a knife sticking in the wall. What's going on over there?"

"We've had a bit of an incident here." A hysterical giggle Zita managed to control simmered beneath the surface.

"An incident? According to Alastair it was more like a war zone with police and an ambulance," Jim continued. "Of course, I recognized her description of Zinnia, a weird woman with red-streaked blond hair. And why would she insult Chrystal?"

A nervous twitter escaped Zita's lips.

"And they did mention your giggling hysterically," Jim said, his tone accusing.

"Jim, I'm exhausted. I don't want to talk now. I'll have Roger come by and explain everything. Chrystal and Alastair are still welcome to stay here. The shootout at the Stillman's Corral is over. Jodie's violent ex-husband was the only casualty."

"Were you or Kimmy injured?" Jim asked.

Zita judged him more than a little late in asking that question. "We're fine now. Thanks for asking. I'm grateful Roger was here. He saved our lives."

"I'm sorry, Mom. I'm babbling. Why didn't I come when Chrystal said there was trouble? I've never been there when you needed me. But you've always been there for me."

Zita heard the line click and then silence. Jim had hung up. It was obvious the MacKinnons didn't have a good impression of her. The memory of them as they fled made her lips twitch. She had to gain control over this inappropriate giggling.

Kimmy entered the kitchen carrying Kyla. "Who was on the phone?"

"Jim. Chrystal and Alastair reported the crisis here in detail." Zita took the ice pack from the freezer and held it to the back of her head. The phone rang again. "I'm not answering. Everyone in town will want their own firsthand account. We need to disconnect the phone. If it's important, family can use our cellphone numbers."

The image of the blood on the breezeway carpet and the mark in the wall were burned into Zita's memory. "I'm going to lie down for an hour. Lock the door, reporters might show up. We're not open for the rest of today." Tears filled her eyes. Exhausted and unnerved, she fled the room.

On her bed, Zita tossed fitfully, unable to block all the swirling dilemmas. Her family remained under suspicion for Clive's murder. And now Brandy had vanished during her stay at their bed-and-breakfast. Brandy was a reporter investigating Clive's body being found in the fish crib. Did Brandy's disappearance make her family appear even guiltier?

Hearing the rumble of voices, male voices, Zita sat up. The

ice pack had caused the swelling to recede but left her feeling damp and chilled. Getting up slowly, she tiptoed toward the kitchen. Kimmy sat at the table holding Kyla. Jim stood in the kitchen doorway.

"Mom, are you all right?" Jim asked. "Kimmy explained everything to me. You could have been killed." He hurried to his mom and wrapped his arms gently around her. "I'm sorry for the way I acted on the phone. Chrystal and Alastair were upsetting Heather. I wanted them out of the hotel."

"I'm fine now that I've had some rest," Zita said. "And don't blame the MacKinnons. I can't imagine how I'd react walking into an unexpected dangerous situation like that."

Zita noticed movement in the breezeway. "Who's here?" She pulled away from Jim.

"Daniel's here, Mom."

Zita walked to the kitchen door. Remembering the blood-soaked carpet made her tremble. Unable to prevent herself, she glanced down. The stain was gone. The carpet was damp but not with blood. "Daniel?"

"Are you feeling better?" Daniel asked. He carried a bucket, sponge mop, and container of carpet cleaner into the garage.

Zita nodded as tears filled her eyes. The damage the knife had done to the paneling had been patched with wood putty. These wonderful friends and family members were a blessing.

"You had quite a ruckus here," Daniel said, returning to the breezeway. "Are you sure you're okay?"

"Yes. It wasn't until it registered that Jodie or Roger might have been killed that I fell apart. What is happening? My life has been chaos since last fall. How can I make it stop?"

Daniel gathered her into his arms. She rested against his shoulder. So many years had passed since a man had comforted her. Tears flowed down her cheeks.

"I've learned that life flows in cycles. We may not understand, but God is in control," Daniel said. "Even in the short time I've been back in Arbor Vale, it's obvious people trust you,

Zita. They come to you for help. God has given you that gift."

Zita stepped back, embarrassed by his words and her weakness. She wiped at her eyes with the back of her hand. "The problem is this thing you call a gift is putting the people I love in danger. And that has to stop."

"You've helped a lot of people recently," Daniel continued. "And God has protected you and your family."

Zita didn't want to dwell on the losses of the past months. She pointed to the wall and then the floor. "Thank you for cleaning and repairing the reminders of this afternoon. I didn't want customers arriving before I had a chance to remove the bloodstain."

When Daniel smiled, his eyes crinkled. "You're welcome. Glad I was able to help."

"How are Deirdre, and the twins, Aubrey and Alexis doing this weekend?" Zita asked, changing the subject to a pleasant topic.

"The camp is going great. We had a bonfire last night at my house on the lake," Daniel said. "They had a blast making s'mores and playing flashlight tag. Ruby and Pearl are giving them a knitting class this afternoon."

"Is Deirdre adjusting?" Zita asked.

"I wish you could have seen how happy she was when the new clothes arrived," Daniel said. "Aubrey and Alexis were excited for Deirdre. They all loved the matching T-shirts and sweatshirts that said Arbor Vale. Thank you, Zita that was very generous."

Someone pounded on the door. Zita jumped. Her nerves hadn't recovered from Trace's invasion earlier.

"Zinnia's here," Daniel said. "Are you up to having more company?"

"Did you really think we could keep her out?" Zita went to unlock the door.

Zinnia rushed in, flushed and agitated. "Hi, Daniel." She halted, eyeing the carpet and the wall. "Oh, that was fast. You really cleaned up the mess."

"I have Daniel to thank for that," Zita said. "What brings you out?"

"It's Saturday and we closed the beauty shop early. I wanted to make sure you were okay. Besides I have some amazing news to share," Zinnia announced.

Kimmy and Jim joined the group in the breezeway. Jim was carrying Kyla.

"I need to practice," Jim said, shifting Kyla to his other shoulder. "Twins." He grinned broadly.

Zita smiled, reflecting on what a balancing act and challenge two babies would be. She shifted her attention to Zinnia. "News? I hope it's good news."

"It is," Zinnia answered. "I'm a finalist in a contest."

"What kind of contest?" Kimmy asked.

Being the center of attention suited Zinnia. She struck a dramatic pose, hands on her hips. "Why a beauty product contest, of course. If I win, I'm going to be on one of those reality shows on television."

Zinnia on television produced all sorts of odd images in Zita's mind. All of them alarming. Zinnia's hair color choices were flamboyant at best and other times plain outrageous. "When did all this happen?"

"If you ever came to the beauty shop you'd know I have secret recipes for hair care." Zinnia said. "They are my most popular products."

"What secret recipes?" Kimmy asked.

Zinnia rolled her eyes. "Do you remember when I was dating Harvey Dekker last fall? He wrote all the wonderful books on flora and fauna in the north woods. Harvey taught me how many plants native to our area have been used in natural beauty products for centuries."

"You never mentioned these products or the contest," Zita said.

"I repeat, Zita, you never come to the beauty shop," Zinnia

huffed. "I didn't mention the contest, because I never expected things to go this far. Apparently they had a representative come in secretly for an appointment. She experimented with all the products I've created and concluded I'd make a great addition to their show. Someone from the production staff contacted me this morning."

"How exciting for you. What happens now?" Zita asked, realizing Zinnia was exactly the type of contestant any reality show would want. Her friend was eccentric and colorful.

"When will you find out if you've been selected?" Kimmy asked.

Zinnia's mouth spread into an irresistible grin. She clasped her hands together and gave an excited little bounce. "They'll call sometime next week. I can hardly wait."

Zita was speechless. What a wonderful adventure for her friend.

"Congratulations, Zinnia," Daniel said. "We'll celebrate your success. My treat. You decide, Zinnia, Mexican, Chinese buffet, or hamburgers?"

"Oh, what fun," Zinnia said. "Definitely Chinese."

"Why not save the rest of our conversation for the restaurant," Daniel said. "Zita hasn't eaten since breakfast, and I can tell she's starting to fade."

"I don't want to spoil the celebration," Zita said. "But with all that's happened, I'm not up to facing the inevitable questions from everyone. Especially if reporters track me down."

"Not a problem," Daniel said. "I'll get carryout." He turned toward Jim. "Will you and Heather join us?"

"Better not, I need to get back to the hotel. Heather can't deal with her parents alone. And there isn't anyone to handle guests arriving."

"There needs to be a schedule at the hotel," Zita said. "We'll need to hire part-time help and someone willing to be on call. You and Heather can't be there 24/7."

Jim walked over and kissed his mother's cheek. "Have to run.

I do have a few people to contact for part-time work." He kissed Zinnia's cheek also. "Be sure and let me know if you win. Congratulations again."

Jim would have to face the dreaded MacKinnons. Zita hoped his in-laws had calmed down by now.

"Torkel's Treasures still isn't open," Zinnia said. "Maybe Roger should do a safety check at their home and business?"

"I'd give them another day," Kimmy said. "I'll mention something to Roger. He might ask around in case they mentioned being away to someone."

Zita agreed with Kimmy—maybe the Torkels were away on business. With a shudder, she eyed the damp spot on the carpet. She'd experienced enough fear and danger for one day. Time to forget the Torkels, Trace, and Brandy for a few hours.

✿⤙ ⤚✿

After their late lunch, Daniel invited Zita to join him and help with a barbeque at his lake home. "You need a few hours away," he said. "And you'll enjoy spending time with the girls. Their enthusiasm will cheer you up. And I want you to see how only one day has transformed Deirdre. She's a perfect example of why I wanted to start this camping opportunity."

Zita agreed that fresh air and children were exactly what she needed. Spending the evening at Daniel's home would get her away from all the nosey phone calls, too. With a brief stop at the hotel, she would have an opportunity to apologize to the MacKinnons for the unfortunate catastrophic mess they had stumbled into. Maybe they'd consider returning to the bed-and-breakfast. Heather didn't need the constant stress their visit created.

When Zita and Daniel entered the hotel, they saw Chrystal sobbing on the loveseat in the lobby. Heather sat next to her, patting her mother's hand. Poor Alastair paced up and down in front of the reception desk.

Zita wondered if the problems at her house were the cause of Chrystal's hysteria. "I came to apologize for the unfortunate incident at my home. I hope you'll reconsider and come back to stay at our bed-and-breakfast."

Alastair stopped pacing and Chrystal managed to stop crying. Jim stepped out of the apartment looking perplexed.

"Twins," Chrystal wailed. "My baby is having twins." She flung herself on Heather's shoulder.

What's her problem, Zita wondered. *Apparently not the chaos at my house. Grandchildren?*

"Chrystal and Alastair will be staying here," Jim announced. "One of our guests checked out. So we have a vacancy."

Zita wondered how her son would cope with his in-laws underfoot. Were they staying to convince Heather and Jim to move back east? "Not getting involved," she whispered under her breath.

"I didn't expect you again today, Mom. Is everything all right at home?" Jim acknowledged Daniel with a nod.

"Everything is fine," Zita said. "I wanted to come by and apologize for the turmoil earlier. We were caught up in a domestic dispute." She wished she could reassure them that it wouldn't happen again. But the way one crisis after another had swirled around her in recent months, the lack of chaos was something she couldn't promise.

"Jim explained everything," Chrystal gushed, smiling. She stood and walked over to Zita and hugged her. "Isn't it marvelous news? Grandbabies! You must be as excited as I am."

Who was this woman and what did she do with Chrystal, Zita wondered. Alastair nodded his head like one of those bobble-headed statues. Heather lifted her shoulders in an exaggerated shrug. The poor girl looked as confused as Zita felt.

Zita took a step back from Chrystal. "New life is a blessing. Twins will be a double blessing."

Movement on the second floor drew Zita's attention. Jenna

came down the stairs followed by Aubrey and Alexis. Bounding down the staircase, the two little girls were smiling.

"We're going out to Uncle Daniel's for a barbeque," Aubrey announced.

"He's going to teach us how to fish," Alexis chimed in.

They wore the matching sweatshirts that Zita had bought for them. She noticed

Deirdre hadn't followed the twins down the stairs. Where was she?

※✕ ✕※

Deirdre ran her hand over the new sweatshirt. She smiled. These were the first pretty new clothes she had ever owned. People gave her things, especially the teachers at school, but those clothes were usually worn and sometimes even dirty.

She wiggled her toes in the tennis shoes. They fit perfectly. Not too tight or floppy. She'd have to hide these things at home or her mom might sell them for drugs. She wondered if the police had taken her mom to jail again. Would Jenna make her go to another foster home? She shuddered. Sometimes that was worse than being with her mom.

The twins, Aubrey and Alexis were nice. That surprised Deirdre. She expected the same treatment she received at school, teasing and hurtful names. They were happy for her, admiring the new clothes.

And for the first time in weeks, she wasn't hungry all the time. So much food and she was allowed to eat as much as she wanted.

Deirdre studied herself in the mirror over the dresser. She hardly recognized the girl reflected back at her. When had she been this clean and smelled like perfume? The condemned house they moved into recently didn't have running water or heat. It wasn't much better than when they lived in their car.

When Mom and her boyfriend fought on Friday, the police came again. That's why Jenna, had taken her away for the weekend. But did she have to go back?

Jenna had braided everyone's hair this morning. Deirdre flipped the French braid over her shoulder. Her hair was shiny and smelled good.

The scarf she had started to knit lay on the bed. The yarn was so soft and pink. Deirdre wondered if she would be able to finish it at home. Those two old ladies who had taught them had been so nice and they baked good cookies. She touched her pocket where she had hidden one for later. At school she often hid food in her pockets. There was rarely anything to eat in the house.

"Deirdre, we're ready to go back to Uncle Daniel's. Come on down!" Jenna called up the stairs from the lobby.

With a final glance in the mirror, Deirdre smiled. She had always been able to take care of herself. This place and these people were better than anything at home. She'd find a way to stay and never go back.

Zita gasped in surprise when Deirdre came down the stairs. She didn't recognize her as the same child who had arrived the previous day. Daniel had used the word transformed. This was a total transformation. Deirdre radiated joy.

Deirdre walked across the lobby to Zita and wrapped her arms around Zita's waist. "Thank you for the new clothes. They're the nicest I've ever had."

"You're very welcome, sweetie," Zita replied, returning the hug. She could only imagine the life this child had been forced to endure. Tears threatened. Her heart hurt for not only Deirdre, but all children who went without adequate food and clothing.

Daniel cleared his throat. "Those hamburgers and hotdogs aren't going to cook themselves. And I'm sure there are some fish waiting to be caught."

Jenna herded the girls toward the door.

"Have fun!" Jim called after the departing group.

"We should get better acquainted," Chrystal said to Zita. "Maybe you could show me around your little town tomorrow afternoon. That would give us a chance to shop and have a nice little chat over a cup of coffee somewhere."

Zita froze. Was this an offer of friendship? Or would it be another snide attack on Arbor Vale, intended to entice Jim and Heather to move back to New York City? She didn't trust Chrystal's motives. Chrystal and Alastair had been alienated from their daughter for ten years. All because Heather had married her son. Zita's anger simmered. She was having trouble controlling her resentment toward the MacKinnons. "I'll call you after church, Chrystal. We can set up a time."

"That will be perfect," Chrystal said.

They exchanged polite smiles.

❋〔 〕❋

Zita rode with Daniel. Jenna had the three girls in the car with her. Zita slumped back in the seat and relaxed. She was thankful that things had calmed down at the hotel. Maybe shopping with Chrystal wouldn't be too bad.

"You're awfully quiet. Are you worried?" Daniel asked.

A little confused, she asked, "About?"

Daniel chuckled. "That's a long list: Deirdre, Heather, Jim, and the babies, the MacKinnons, Brandy, Jodie, Clive..."

"Stop!" Zita cried. "Enough. I don't need to be reminded. And that's only half the list. What's that word... quagmire? That list is my own personal quagmire."

"For the last two miles you've been gnawing on something," Daniel said. "Why are you fretting?"

"Chrystal," Zita answered. "I find it hard to believe she's

140

changed that much in one afternoon. Especially after choosing to ignore Heather and Jim all these years."

Daniel turned into his driveway and parked. "Babies are little miracles. They change lives and attitudes. You should know that, Grandma."

Zita couldn't stop the grin that spread across her face. *Grandma.* She loved the sound of that word.

Jenna pulled into the driveway behind Daniel. Car doors slammed. The three girls raced past Daniel's car, running toward the lake, yelling and laughing. Grinning at their antics, Jenna trotted behind.

"We'd better get cookin'," Daniel said. "Those kids will be ready to eat soon. We'll have another bonfire tonight. They were attentive during the Bible study last night and asked great questions. Especially Deirdre."

Zita followed Daniel around to the back of his beautiful log home. She noticed that the sprayed graffiti from last February had been removed and the logs restored. For now the resistance to Daniel's camp had died down. She hoped the Torkels' efforts to prevent these children from coming had been completely defeated.

"Jenna, do you need any help?" Daniel called. "If not, Zita and I will get supper started."

Jenna waved, acknowledging she could handle the girls.

"Since I remodeled things for the camp, you haven't had a chance to see the improvements inside," Daniel said, offering Zita his arm as they climbed the steps.

When Zita rested her hand on Daniel's arm, her heart beat faster. She loved this kind, selfless man. *Love.* The word caused her to misstep and stumble. Heat rose in her cheeks.

Daniel steadied her. "Watch your step."

CHAPTER THIRTEEN

Daniel gave Zita a quick tour of his home. As they stepped inside, her memories filtered back to the last time she had been in Daniel's home. His parents had hosted a small party for friends and family after their high school graduation. The names and faces from nearly fifty years ago slipped through her memory. She smiled, recalling that carefree time in her life. Daniel left for college that summer and didn't return until this past year.

The Edwards' log home remained rustic and cozy. The large eat-in kitchen had a pine table and benches that could easily seat twelve people. Daniel led Zita into the living room. A huge natural stone fireplace covered one wall. A large picture window overlooked the lake. An assortment of comfortable chairs and a sofa in shades of woodland brown and forest green created a comfy, welcoming setting.

"This room is perfect for gathering your campers together in the evening," Zita said. "I can picture meaningful conversations and instruction taking place."

Daniel pointed toward a doorway at the back corner of the room. "Last stop on this floor is the master bedroom."

Zita followed Daniel into a room filled with a mixture of

heavy, dark wooden furniture and Northwood's décor. *Definitely masculine.*

They returned to the living room and climbed the staircase to the loft. The space held four sets of bunk beds, several dressers, a walk-in closet, and a large bathroom.

"I've installed extra showers in this bathroom, there's another one on the main floor, plus a locker room in the basement. Everything's in place, if only I could get approval. And I doubt the Torkels will ever back down." Daniel sighed. "We'd better move along. I need to start the grill; those kids are going to be hungry. We'll save the basement for another time."

"This is perfect for your camp," Zita said. "I don't wish any misfortune for the Torkels. But it would be wonderful if they've decided to move away."

Daniel started to descend the stairs. "That would make my life easier."

Once again in the kitchen, Daniel set out the ground beef and hotdogs. Zita assembled ketchup, mustard, relish, and carrot sticks. They worked well together.

"Have you ever considered marrying again?" Daniel asked.

The knife Zita was using to slice tomatoes slipped from her fingers, clattering onto the counter. She didn't have an answer to his question. She found Daniel watching her reaction intently. Heat rose in her cheeks.

Gradually she managed to form a two-word question of her own. "Have you?"

"Not until recently," he answered. "Careful with that knife; I don't want you cutting your finger. I'm going out to start the grill."

Zita watched him leave with her mouth open. *Marry again? Recently?* She put both hands to her hot cheeks, wondering if he meant... exactly what? Her thoughts churned in uncertainty. Had Daniel decided to marry again? Who? An upsetting question washed over her: What if he meant someone other than her? After all, they had always been just good friends. Picking up the knife, her hand shook.

When Daniel returned, the subject of marriage wasn't mentioned again. A decision was reached to eat inside rather than at the picnic table. The early evening had turned chilly and damp. Daniel started a fire in the fireplace, giving a cheery glow to the house. As they ate, laughter and chatter flowed easily around the table.

After the meal, paper plates and cups were tossed into the fire. Zita wished cleaning up after all meals was this simple.

They gathered around the fireplace for a Bible story and lesson. While listening to Daniel's expressive voice, Zita curled up in a chair and studied him. She noted how he held everyone's attention. As he spoke, his eyes sparkled with enjoyment, a born story teller. He leaned forward, resting his elbows on his knees, listening intently to Deirdre's question. He looked in Zita's direction, a warm smile tipping up the corners of his mouth.

Zita's heart skipped a beat. His smile felt as intimate as a kiss. But she was no longer a teenager with some silly crush. When Daniel returned this year, it was as if he had never been away. They had a history and friendship to build on. But if they moved forward with a relationship and failed, their friendship might be permanently damaged.

With a deep sign, she forced her attention to return to the girls. They apparently decided to forgo the fishing this late in the day and opted instead for the game room in the basement.

During the next few hours, the recreation room held laughter and music. Daniel's sound system played every Sunday school song Zita had ever learned. Between games of *Go Fish* and *Old Maid*, they sang along.

At first, Deirdre seemed confused by the games and the singing. But she caught on quickly and was soon winning games and singing loudly while doing motions to the songs.

The evening ended too quickly. The girls were moaning and groaning because they had to return home the next day after church.

Daniel offered them a return visit during summer vacation for a longer stay. "Next time we'll be able to swim, learn to fish, and do some hiking."

Standing quietly off to the side, Deirdre remained silent. Would she be sent back into her horrible family situation? Zita decided to take Jenna aside tomorrow and ask her what would happen to Deirdre.

"Thank you, Daniel, for a wonderful evening," Zita said. "This is exactly what I needed."

He cupped her elbow with his hand. "I'm driving you home."

She hesitated. "Don't bother. Jenna can drop me off on the way to the hotel."

"It's not a bother, and I am driving you home." His tone left no room for further discussion.

Zita's insides did a nervous flutter but she didn't argue.

Still holding her arm, Daniel walked with her to his truck and held the door for her. Zita couldn't relax. Alone with Daniel, her nerves were jittery. To Zita, their usual easy camaraderie had evaporated. Her hands were clenched tight in her lap.

They drove in silence for a few minutes. Then Daniel discussed the girls and in particular Deirdre. "Jenna has been in contact with her office to locate suitable placement for Deirdre. There are other foster care options, but locating family is the first choice."

"I hope there is a positive solution. That little girl deserves the proper care and most of all, love," Zita said, relieved that they had found common ground for a conversation.

When they pulled into her driveway and parked, Daniel turned toward her and asked, "I answered your question earlier. Do you have an answer for me?"

Zita realized what he was asking and her only answer was the same as his. "Not until recently. Very recently."

Daniel threw back his head and laughed.

❋✵ ✵❋

Sunday morning, Zita anticipated a quiet time of worship at church. Heather and Jim came in with Chrystal and Alastair, who wore brittle half-smiles. The foursome sat down directly in front of Zita. Chrystal lost no time in leaning over the back of the pew.

"You will call me this afternoon so we can shop and chat," Chrystal ordered rather than asked.

Zita nodded and returned to concentrating on her bulletin. She continued to wonder what had caused Chrystal's sudden chumminess. The woman apparently had an agenda. If nothing else, Zita's quiet Sunday afternoon would be ruined.

When Jodie Chatwyn and Kenneth Hardgrave walked into the church, a flurry of whispers arose. Makeup did little to disguise Jodie's black eye and swollen lip. Zita flinched. This was exactly what Arbor Vale didn't need, more grist for the rumor mill. But she was thankful to see them turning to God in the midst of all the turmoil in their lives.

A few minutes later, Roger, Carter, Kimmy, and Kyla arrived, joining Zita.

Jenna entered with the three girls, causing more whispered chatter. As Aubrey, Alexis, and Deirdre walked down the aisle, they were all smiles, waving at Zita.

Daniel materialized next to Zita. With a smile and a nod, he sat down next to her. Zita's pulse skittered erratically.

When Zinnia arrived, she forced Daniel to squeeze closer to Zita. Zinnia smiled and fluttered her eyelashes at Daniel.

Romance and intrigue swarmed around Zita. She worried how Zinnia might react if a more-than-friends relationship developed between herself and Daniel. Obviously, Zinnia was attracted to him. But then, Zinnia was interested in every handsome male of a certain age.

When the organist began playing, the congregation quieted. Zita struggled to concentrate on the hymns and the pastor's sermon. Her thoughts flitted from Suzanne Chatwyn's funeral the next day to the missing Brandy Gardell and Clive's still unsolved murder. And this afternoon she would say good-bye to Jenna and the girls. Her heart remained heavy over Deirdre's future.

When the service ended, Chrystal gripped Zita's wrist. "You'll pick me up at the hotel in an hour."

Spending even five minutes with Chrystal would give Zita a headache or maybe an ulcer. This was a woman who gave orders and expected them to be obeyed.

Clinging to Daniel's arm, Zinnia asked, "Do you have plans for lunch? Why not come back to my house?"

"Do you have plans, Zita?" Daniel asked.

Zinnia glared at Zita. The message was, "Don't you dare."

Zinnia's possessive expression and Daniel's distressed one pushed Zita into a full-blown headache. Perplexed by all the mixed messages, she wished she could help Daniel out of this predicament. But she had been forced into other plans.

"She won't have time," Chrystal interrupted. "Zita promised to show me around your little town of Arbor Vale."

The pronouncement made Zinnia's grin wider.

"I need to finalize several things with the weekend campers," Daniel said, sounding apologetic. "They'll be returning home in a few hours. Why don't you join our group for lunch, Zinnia? We're having pizza, and I'm sure the girls will enjoy spending time with you."

"I suppose I could," Zinnia said, going into a pout.

"You'll need to come to the hotel to meet Chrystal, so why not join us, Zita?" Daniel suggested.

Zinnia's frown deepened. But Zita decided it was foolish to refuse. She'd be able to say good-bye to Jenna and the girls, spend time with Daniel, and be ready for her excursion with Chrystal.

"I'd like that," Zita replied. But between Zinnia's stormy expression and Chrystal's tightening grip on her arm, it was as though she had been strapped to the rack and was being pulled apart.

✻⤙ ⤚✻

The tangy aroma of pepperoni and pizza sauce met Zita at the door of the hotel. Her taste buds tingled. Zinnia, Chrystal, and Alastair were in the apartment at the back of the lobby. Jenna had spread a blanket on the kitchen floor. Alexis, Aubrey, and Deirdre were having their own picnic.

Zita ended up trapped at the table between Zinnia, who continued to scowl and sulk, and Chrystal, who yammered on and on about her society friends and events in New York.

Meanwhile Daniel sat down with his campers on the floor. Jim and Heather joined them.

"How do you fix a broken pizza?" Daniel asked. When no one came up with an answer, he said, "Tomato paste." Giggling over Daniel's silly joke, the girls continued to eat their lunch.

The pizza Zita managed to swallow formed a doughy lump in her stomach. Unable to concentrate on Chrystal's running commentary, she zoned out, lost in her own thoughts and oblivious to everyone and everything around her.

Alastair, absorbed in the *Wall Street Journal*, would grunt occasionally in reply to a question from Chrystal which required his response.

"Are you ready to have our little shopping trip?" Chrystal asked, poking Zita in the arm, bringing her out of her reverie.

"I'll say good-bye to the girls first," Zita said, covering her uneaten pizza with a napkin.

Tears stung Zita's eyes as she hugged Deirdre. She wondered what would happen to this sweet child.

"Call me later," Zinnia ordered Daniel.

Daniel gave a brief shake of his head before rewarding Zita with an understanding smile. Amusement flickered in his eyes. Zita hoped at the end of this day, she would find humor in this situation.

Once again, Chrystal clamped unto Zita's wrist and tugged her toward the door. All Zita wanted to do was shake this woman off and go home to Kimmy and Kyla. But she needed to do this for Heather and Jim and hopefully keep the peace.

While Zita drove, Chrystal kept up a steady stream of questions. Some of them were pushing the boundaries of polite conversation. "Your niece lives with you and you operate a small business out of your home?"

Zita nodded, keeping her eyes on the road.

"How can you afford to own a hotel?" Chrystal probed.

Rude. "I inherited the hotel from my aunt." Zita hoped the inquisition had ended.

"I understand it has quite the colorful past." Crystal's comment bordered on sarcasm with more than a hint of innuendo. "Your aunt was the original owner?"

Irritation consumed Zita. *Enough.* "My aunt bought the hotel so that Pearl and Ruby Gem would have a place to live. Those two dear elderly sisters are the daughters of the original owner."

"Really? I can't imagine why your aunt would do that."

Chrystal's attitude didn't surprise Zita. The woman came across as totally self-absorbed. "We're a small community, and we take care of each other." Zita couldn't resist a small jibe. "You probably wouldn't understand that, living in a large city."

Chrystal's eyes narrowed and her mouth hardened into a straight line.

Realizing she had struck a nerve, Zita wasn't successful in preventing the mischievous smile twitching at the corners of her mouth.

Noting a parking place on the main street, Zita pulled in. "Did you have anything in particular you wanted to shop for?"

"I plan to get some special things for my grandchildren," Chrystal gushed. "What have you purchased for them?"

Zita exited the car and met Chrystal on the sidewalk. "I'm waiting for Heather and Jim to choose a theme for their nursery."

"What could they possibly comprehend about quality or

popular motif? Alastair and I will have our decorator design the nursery," Chrystal continued, viewing the storefront window display and ignoring Zita.

This was Chrystal's real agenda for the outing. Zita stiffened her spine. Her stomach muscles clenched.

"My daughter wasn't raised and educated for *this* kind of life!"

"What kind of life is that?" Zita asked. She refused to make this insulting conversation easy for Chrystal. "Are you referring to marriage, motherhood, or operating a business? I've found your daughter to be quite resourceful in all those areas."

With a huff of displeasure, Chrystal put her hands on her hips. "That's not what I meant. Heather was raised to take her place in society." She disdainfully glanced around. "I won't allow my grandchildren to be raised in this, this backwoods settlement."

Zita expected the woman to start stamping her foot. Controlling her anger, she kept her voice calm. "You won't allow? Heather and Jim are adults and more than capable of making their own decisions. And that includes where and how they want to raise their children."

"Don't you want what's best for them and our grandchildren?" Chrystal's voice grew louder. "Apparently not."

"Enough." Zita's fingers curled into her palms. The nails dug into the soft flesh. "For someone expressing all this concern, where were you the last ten years? Or even the last month when their lives fell apart and they had nowhere to go? How dare you try to manipulate their lives now."

"You wouldn't understand. How could you, living as you do. People getting shot in your home." Chrystal gave a derisive laugh. "That's where you want our grandchildren to be raised. I heard a body was found in your lake. Some believe your husband killed him or even Jim."

Starting to shake, Zita clamped her mouth tight until her jaws ached.

"Zita, your cell phone must be off!" someone shouted. "We need you."

She turned. Daniel was double parked next to her car. Anger slid quickly into fear. Something was wrong.

"Deirdre's gone. We're searching for her," Daniel called.

Zita took her car keys and tossed them to Chrystal. "I'm needed elsewhere," she said. "Enjoy your shopping."

Chrystal for once remained speechless, her mouth hanging open.

As Daniel drove toward the hotel, he explained to Zita what had happened. "The girls were packing their things to leave. Deirdre carried her duffel down to the lobby and vanished."

The possibilities of what could have happened to Deirdre tore through Zita. "Could her mother have come and taken her?"

Daniel gave a sharp shrug of his shoulders. "Anything is possible, but we assume she ran away."

"Ran away? Why would she do that?" As the words left her mouth, Zita already knew the answer. "The poor little thing is probably afraid to go home. She was safe and happy here." Worry, ragged and painful, caused a tightening in her chest.

The Sunday afternoon traffic through town continued in a heavy stream. Tourists were heading home from their weekend retreats. Keeping his attention on the road, Daniel nodded.

"Who's out searching for her? Did you call Roger?" Zita asked.

"When I left the hotel to find you, Roger was organizing a search," Daniel explained. "Jim and Heather volunteered to drive Alexis and Aubrey home. The twins staged a protest over leaving without Deirdre. Jenna is remaining until Deirdre is found."

When Zita and Daniel arrived, Zinnia, Kimmy, and Kyla were already at the hotel. Jenna paced frantically in front of the reception desk. "I should have expected this," she wailed.

"This isn't your fault." Zita gathered Jenna into a hug.

"But I'm responsible for the girls in my care." Jenna dabbed at her eyes. "Where would she go?"

"Deirdre couldn't have gotten far on foot," Kimmy said. "She's a smart little girl. She'll realize running away won't solve anything."

"Take these and pass them out." Daniel handed out flyers of what Deirdre was wearing and describing her duffel bag. "Roger led a group to the outskirts of town and the parks. He wanted us to stay in town. Let's divide up the four blocks near the hotel into teams of two."

"I'm with Daniel," Zinnia chirped, latching on to his arm.

"Auntie and I will search together," Kimmy offered.

Gently untangling his arm from Zinnia's, Daniel said, "Jenna, this is difficult, but you need to stay at the hotel. If Deirdre comes back, contact Roger. If his team finds her, he'll be in touch with you."

Zita understood the strain of waiting. As the seconds ticked by, fear crept in. She squeezed Jenna's hand but wasn't able to offer words of encouragement.

Daniel offered a prayer for Deirdre and each volunteer. His words calmed Zita and gave her confidence that they would find Deirdre safe.

Daniel and Zinnia took the south side of the street. Zita and Kimmy, pushing Kyla in a stroller, visited each business to the north. Each stop used up valuable minutes. Many shops had already closed early on this Sunday afternoon. Doors and windows had to be examined for any sign of a break-in. They left a flyer with Deirdre's description at the businesses that were open. An hour passed and Zita and Kimmy hadn't even completed the first street.

Kyla's happy baby babble changed to a loud complaint of "ma-ma-ma."

"Somebody needs a diaper change and a drink," Kimmy said. "I left her juice and snack in the hotel refrigerator."

"I'm fine on my own," Zita said. "Take care of our little girl."

"I'll catch up with you in a few minutes," Kimmy said as she crossed the street.

Zita moved on to the next shop. Out of the corner of her eye, she noticed a shadow of movement down near Torkel's Treasures. *Odd.* Wondering if that was Deirdre or if Beatrice and Floyd had returned, Zita hurried off in that direction.

The building was dark and silent. Zita pounded on the front door before moving around to the side of the store. There she pushed on a window, which was locked tight. A large panel van was tucked back in a tree-shaded area partially hidden from view. Several large packing crates were stacked next to the vehicle.

Assuming the Torkels had returned, Zita walked up to the door and called, "Beatrice! Floyd! Are you here?" When no one responded, she worried that she might have carelessly stepped into a robbery. Slowly she backed away from the door.

"Zita, is that you?" Beatrice asked from inside the dark store. She came and stood in the doorway. "What do you want?"

Beatrice's appearance had deteriorated during her absence. She looked haggard, her hair and clothing unkempt.

"Are you feeling all right?" Zita asked. She wondered if something had happened to Floyd. "We've wondered why your store hasn't been open."

"Why are you here?" Beatrice demanded, ignoring Zita's question.

Obviously the woman's personality hadn't improved. Zita held out the flyer. "This little girl is missing. We've been stopping at all the buildings in town."

Beatrice smirked. "Must be one of Daniel's little campers. Something like this was bound to happen. She's probably breaking into businesses as we speak and stealing everything in sight. I warned everyone not to allow those delinquents in our town." She scowled, glancing back into the dark interior of the store.

Angered by Beatrice's prejudice, Zita replied, "These children are only eight or nine years old."

"In the cities criminal behavior starts young," Beatrice

snapped.

Choosing to ignore the woman's comments, Zita returned to the important task of finding Deirdre. "Has your door been unlocked or the store unattended for any length of time?" she asked, peering around Beatrice. "Would you mind if I checked inside for Deirdre?"

Beatrice moved squarely in front of Zita, blocking the doorway. "I most certainly would. Floyd and I would know if someone were in the store."

A muffled cry echoed out from the dim interior. "What's that? Deirdre might be inside and injured." Angry with Beatrice's attitude, Zita lunged past her, colliding with Floyd.

Arms tightened around Zita, shoving her to the floor. It only took a few seconds for her to be bound with rope and duct tape pasted across her mouth. She was confused and terrified. Her stomach roiled.

"Nosy, helpful Zita," Beatrice snarled. She kicked Zita.

Pain jolted through Zita's back where it smacked into the edge of a counter. She moaned.

A malicious giggle came from Beatrice. She lifted her foot to kick Zita again.

Zita gritted her teeth, waiting for the blow to land.

"Leave her!" Floyd yelled. "We need to get the rest of this stuff loaded and get out of here permanently. Move."

When Beatrice stalked away, Zita slumped forward. She tested the ropes binding her. They didn't budge. She feared for Deirdre's safety. What if the little girl was a prisoner as well? Had that earlier cry been her?

The Torkels continued to move through the store, packing and carrying out boxes. Zita had trouble understanding what was going on. Why had they attacked her? The nightmarish situation was insane at best. The weak moan she heard earlier echoed again in the murky store interior.

"Use that stuff and shut them both up," Floyd snarled.

When Zita heard Beatrice's footsteps coming toward her, stark terror lasted only seconds. An odd-smelling cloth was slapped across her nose. Zita's last conscious thought was *chloroform.*

CHAPTER FOURTEEN

When Kimmy entered the hotel, Jenna jumped up from the chair in the lobby. "Have you found her?" she asked.

"Sorry, no," Kimmy replied. "Any word from Roger's search team?"

Discouragement and frustration radiated from Jenna. "I called my supervisor to report that Deirdre's missing. On top of everything else, there's good news of a possible placement for her. If only she hadn't run away!"

After lifting Kyla from the stroller, Kimmy walked into the apartment. Jenna followed. "Kyla needed a diaper change and a snack," Kimmy explained, laying Kyla on a blanket on the floor. After giving the baby a bottle of cool water, Kimmy changed her diaper. "Auntie Zita has continued checking the businesses on the first block. I'll catch up with her in a few minutes."

They heard someone enter the hotel. Chrystal had returned from her shopping trip.

"Is anyone here?" Chrystal called.

"Alastair is upstairs in your room," Kimmy answered. "Everyone else is out searching for the missing girl." She wasn't able to keep the annoyance from her voice.

Only Alastair had remained behind, unwilling to help in the search. Ignoring any further interaction with Chrystal, Kimmy returned to the kitchen.

Chrystal came and stood in the doorway. "Where is Heather?"

"Jim and Heather volunteered to drive Alexis and Aubrey home." Kimmy bent and picked up Kyla. The baby gripped her bottle tightly. Adding two teething biscuits to her daughter's diaper bag, Kimmy returned Kyla to the stroller. She was relieved to turn her back on Chrystal and let Jenna handle the self-absorbed woman.

Kimmy walked slowly along the street, searching for Zita. After a few minutes, she reached Torkel's Treasures. She found Floyd in the back of the building loading boxes into a van. "Hi, Mr. Torkel, has my aunt spoken with you?"

Floyd continued loading without acknowledging Kimmy. Beatrice came outside carrying a suitcase. She halted when she noticed Kimmy.

"We're not open for business," Beatrice snapped, continuing on to the van.

"Has my aunt stopped by?" Kimmy asked.

"No," Beatrice replied, her tone abrupt and dismissive.

Following Beatrice, Kimmy held out the flyer. "Have you noticed this little girl?"

After setting down the suitcase next to the van, Beatrice turned back toward Kimmy. "We've been working here all afternoon. And haven't spoken to anyone. We're in a hurry. Have an antique show to attend out of state tomorrow. I don't have time to chat or help find people you've misplaced."

Irritated by the insufferable woman and growing uneasy concerning her aunt's whereabouts, Kimmy turned Kyla's stroller back toward the street. "If my aunt stops by, please tell her to meet me back at the hotel."

Beatrice gave a dismissive shrug. "Whatever."

Kimmy tried to call Zita's cell phone. She hoped her aunt had carried it with her. The phone rang and rang and then went to voice mail. Kimmy became more and more nervous over Zita's absence. She dialed the hotel. "Hi Jenna, has Zita come back or called?"

Jenna reported that she hadn't seen or spoken to anyone.

❊⤳ ⤳❊

The chirping birds inside Zita's head went beyond annoying. She wondered how to make them stop before recognizing the twittering sound came from her cell phone. One eye managed to open. Her mouth and throat were dry. Why couldn't she move? And where was she? The duct tape made it impossible to open her mouth. Counters and display cases came into focus. Memories swarmed with frightening images.

"Beatrice, find the cell phone and shut it off! If that niece hears it, she'll be back with her police boyfriend," Floyd ordered.

The screen door slammed shut and Zita heard footsteps, heading her way. She closed her eyes and relaxed, pretending to still be unconscious. Nausea built in the pit of her stomach. She willed herself not to be sick.

Standing over her, Beatrice rummaged through Zita's purse. She apparently found the phone and turned it off. A few minutes later Beatrice mumbled, "You won't need this cash or your credit cards. They might come in handy."

The purse dropped to the floor, landing inches from Zita's face. She used every ounce of control not to flinch.

Floyd joined Beatrice in the store. "What are we going to do with them?" he asked.

"We'll have more time to escape if we take them with," Beatrice said. "We can dump them when we cross the Flambeau River. It's still running high from winter runoff and recent rains. Could take weeks for the bodies to wash up. With all the tree roots and stuff, they might never surface."

"I'll back the van up to the door. We'll use the cart to load them," Floyd said.

Helplessness and horror threatened to overwhelm Zita. But she needed to find a way to escape. Was Deirdre injured and tied up in the store? Had the little girl wandered into this mess to find a place to hide? Zita determined to remain strong and find a way to rescue them both.

Zita heard a motor start. There were only minutes remaining to find a way to end this madness. She wouldn't allow herself to dwell on the possibility of drowning in the river. Beatrice was moving around with some sort of wheeled contraption. Zita judged her to be farther back in the store. Wiggling, she worked to loosen the ropes on her wrists, causing them to tear her flesh.

There was movement under one of the display cases in front of Zita. She shivered, imagining some furry creature with teeth. If she made any noise, the Torkels would use the chloroform again and all hope for survival would be lost.

Zita was unable to believe her eyes when Deirdre wiggled out from under the glass display case. She was pale as she crept toward Zita. Deirdre held her finger to her lips. Her small hands worked on the ropes that bound Zita's hands. They loosened slightly, but Beatrice and her cart was coming.

Deirdre leaned in and whispered, "I'll get help." She slithered back under the display case.

Filled with renewed hope, Zita relaxed, pretending to be unconscious. Deirdre was safe. That was what truly mattered. Certain that she had heard someone moan, she pondered who the other victim might be.

The Torkels roughly loaded Zita onto a wheeled cart. As she was tossed and jolted, Zita gathered all her courage and survival instinct to keep from moaning. Her hope rested on an eight-year-old child.

The Torkels tossed Zita forcefully into the back of the van. Her head hit the metal floor. She gritted her teeth to keep from crying out.

The doors slammed shut and soon Beatrice and Floyd were in the front seat, driving out of the parking area. Zita opened her eyes and quietly and carefully worked to loosen her ropes. She studied the slender shape next to her on the floor. Recognition shuddered through her. *Brandy!*

When Deirdre heard the van drive away she wiggled out of her hiding place. Auntie Zita was the kindest person she had ever met, next to Jenna. Even if it meant being sent back to her mother, she had to save her new friend.

Toting her prized duffel bag, Deirdre unlocked the door. She peered outside, making sure those nasty, frightening people had really left. Realizing the hotel was the closest place to get help, she scurried around the corner of the building. As she raced across the street, someone shouted her name. She reached the hotel and pulled open the door, nearly collapsing inside the lobby.

Heart pounding, Deirdre paused to catch her breath. All she managed to gasp out were the words, "Help Auntie Zita. They took her."

Aunt Jenna leapt up from the loveseat and wrapped her arms around her. "Where have you been? Everyone is out looking for you."

Tears trickled down Deirdre's cheeks. Her stomach churned with anxiety and frustration. Aunt Jenna didn't understood how scared she was for Zita. Those horrible people were going to drown her in some river. There had been another woman tied up and unconscious and they planned to kill her too. Her words apparently hadn't registered. She needed to make Aunt Jenna understand. "Auntie Zita needs help!"

Kimmy rushed into the lobby, pushing Kyla in the stroller. "I saw you run across the street from Torkel's Treasures, thank goodness you're safe," she gasped.

Deirdre pulled away from Jenna. "Auntie Zita needs help!" she screamed.

Jenna grabbed her by the shoulders, spinning her around. "What's happened to Zita?"

"They tied her up! They're going to drown her in the river!" Deirdre shrieked. "We need to hurry!"

"Who's going to drown her?" Kimmy gasped.

Daniel and Zinnia returned to the hotel from their search. Daniel said, "Praise the Lord, you're unharmed. We can call off the search." He scanned the room. "Where's Zita?"

Jenna had rushed to the reception desk and was calling Roger and his search team. "Deirdre's back," she said. "But Zita is missing and may have been kidnapped. Hurry!"

Zinnia's face drained of color as she wailed, "What's happened to my cousin?"

Kyla, upset by the commotion, became fussy. Kimmy lifted her from the stroller and bounced her gently on her hip.

Daniel bent down next to Deirdre. "Tell me everything that happened." He kept his voice calm.

The tears continued to flood Deirdre's cheeks. "I didn't want to go back home. I thought if I hid maybe someone would keep me. I went inside a store and hid under some counters. Then some people came and started packing up the store. And then I heard someone. Some woman was tied up near me." She shuddered at the memory of the frightening experience.

"Was it Auntie Zita?" Kimmy asked.

"No," Deirdre answered. "A stranger. But she's sick and moaning."

"Tell us what happened to Auntie Zita," Daniel urged.

"When she came into the store, they knocked her down and tied her up. They used some smelly stuff to make her sleep."

Zinnia wailed louder. "We need to help her." She turned as if to rush off to the store.

"She's not there anymore," Deirdre said. "They took her and the other woman away in their van." She leaned into Daniel and wept on his shoulder. "I couldn't save her. The knots on her hands were too tight. But I loosened them."

"Where were they going?" Daniel asked.

"They said they were going out of state." Deirdre sniffled and straightened, looking directly into Daniel's eyes. "I heard them say they're going to throw Auntie Zita and the other woman into the Flambeau River and drown them."

Zinnia shrieked, placing a hand over her heart. "We have to save them!"

Daniel ignored Zinnia's outburst and hugged Deirdre. "You're a hero. Auntie Zita knows you've gone for help. And you may have loosened her ropes enough for her to work her way free. You were very brave and I'm proud of you."

Deirdre managed a tentative smile.

Roger rushed into the hotel. "Deirdre has been found but now Zita is missing? I've called all the search teams to meet back here. Tell me what's happened."

Daniel reported everything Deirdre had told them.

"Who's the other victim?" Roger asked.

"Could it be Brandy Gardell?" Kimmy asked.

Roger gave a sharp nod. "Might be. Do we have any idea which direction the Torkels are heading? Or what kind of car they were driving?"

Everyone stared at Deirdre. "I was hiding under a counter, I didn't see a car."

"Beatrice and Floyd were loading a white panel van when I stopped to ask them if they had spotted Deirdre," Kimmy said. "Roger, please stop them, they plan to hurt my aunt." She shuddered and Kyla leaned against her mother's shoulder as if sensing she needed comforting.

"I'll issue an all-points bulletin. We can have officers at every river crossing in minutes, setting up road blocks." Roger used his cell phone to start issuing orders.

"What can we do?" Daniel asked.

"Stay put," Roger said. "I'll call as soon as we find them."

Kimmy's stomach roiled with fear and despair. She couldn't just stay at the hotel and not even try to find Zita. She took a step toward Roger. "Can't I—"

"Take care of Kyla," Roger interrupted. "I don't want anyone else to go missing." He hugged Kimmy and kissed her cheek. "Not to worry. We'll find Zita."

After Roger left, Daniel spread out a map across the reception desk, tracing roads with his finger. "I can't sit here and wait, I'm going out to help find Zita. There's a lot of ground to cover. Torkel could be driving north to Canada or south to Mexico."

"They'll go north," Kimmy said. "They'll want to dispose of their victims quickly and leave the country."

Daniel continued to study the map. "I'm checking routes that cross the river. Floyd is familiar with the area; he'll take a back road." His finger stabbed the map. "There." He circled the river crossing with a red pen.

"It isn't safe for you to go alone," Kimmy said. "Roger wanted us to wait here."

Daniel strode toward the door. "We've wasted too much time already. They have a head start."

"I'm going with you!" Zinnia shrieked, grabbing at Daniel's arm.

"No, this is too dangerous." He shook her off. "I will find her."

Every bump in the road jolted Zita. Her arms and hands ached. She scooted nearer to Brandy. The young woman was alive, but her breathing was shallow.

Zita was very aware that their lives rested in the hands of a young girl and the ability of the police to find them. If they reached the river Brandy and she might not survive. The terrifying realization that she might never be with her family again struck like a physical blow. The van grew hot and stuffy. Sweat trickled down her neck. Despair almost overcame her resolute control. She clenched her teeth. The Torkels would not win.

As Zita struggled with the ropes binding her wrists, images of friends and family haunted her. Hope spiked when her fingers managed to reach the loosened knot. She offered a prayer of thanks for Deirdre.

Raised voices erupted from the front seat. Floyd and Beatrice were quarreling. Zita stilled to listen. For once it sounded as though Floyd had found his backbone and was insisting on going to Canada. Beatrice argued that they would be safer in Mexico and she was tired of cold weather. The bickering continued, growing louder.

Under the cover of their yelling, Zita wrestled with her ropes. When her hands broke free, she removed the tape from her mouth and set to work on the ropes binding her ankles. Her fingers ached and tingled, making it difficult to untie the knots. Biting down hard on her lip, she focused on freeing herself.

The voices in the front seat were quiet again. Zita was thankful for the cover all the boxes and crates provided. Free at last, she turned to Brandy. Afraid the woman might wakeup and cry out, Zita left the tape covering Brandy's mouth in place. She untied Brandy's hands first and them her feet.

Zita leaned back down on the floor. Without a plan, freedom meant nothing. Alone, against Beatrice and Floyd, she didn't have a chance.

❀⟡ ⟡❀

Kimmy couldn't decide if she should contact Jim or wait until he and Heather returned from driving Alexis and Aubrey home. He needed to be told what had happened to his mother.

Chrystal came down the stairs. "What's all the commotion? I was resting."

She stared at Deirdre. "You found the missing child."

"My aunt has been kidnapped," Kimmy said. "The Torkels plan to kill her."

Chrystal took a step back up the stairs. "Alastair!" she shouted. "Get up, we're leaving." She glared down at Kimmy. "Insanity runs rampant in this community. I won't allow my grandchildren to be raised here."

"That won't be your decision," Kimmy said tersely.

"How dare you!" Zinnia screeched. "My very best friend in the entire world is in danger. If you weren't Heather's mother I'd throw you out myself." She raised her fist and shook it at the woman.

Chrystal fled up the stairs.

"Good riddance," Zinnia muttered.

Kimmy sat down and rocked Kyla. In a matter of minutes, the baby dozed in her arms. Deirdre curled up next to Jenna. Apparently exhausted from her frightening experience, the child's eyes drifted shut. Only Zinnia continued to pace and mumble. "Why haven't they called? Why haven't they found her yet?"

Zita searched for anything she could use as a weapon against Beatrice and Floyd. Nothing. Helplessness spurted through her. She needed a plan.

As a child, she had learned a magic trick with a rope. Tied to resemble a regular knot, with a slight tug the knot would release. Carefully she wrapped the ropes back around Brandy's ankles and wrists. It wasn't much of a scheme, but it was her only chance.

165

Then she repeated the process on her own ankles and returned the tape to her mouth. Her wrists were harder to manage. Again and again, she worked the rope, unable to slide her hands in and tighten it convincingly.

Zita's worries over Brandy escalated. The young woman remained unconscious, pale and unresponsive.

Beatrice and Floyd were arguing over deserting their lucrative business. Working frantically with the rope, Zita listened to the conversation in the front seat. Apparently the Torkels bought and sold stolen property. They were fences. It sounded as though their illegal activities had gone on profitably for years. She had never liked the Torkels, but criminals? This was difficult for her to process. Yet their confession was undeniable.

When she heard them mention Clive Chatwyn, Zita froze.

"Why after all these years did Clive's body have to be discovered?" Beatrice asked. "But our plan worked. Zita's family was blamed, even if it did take years to happen. If only that reporter woman hadn't shown up."

Zita struggled to grasp the meaning of what Beatrice was saying. The Torkels were responsible for Clive's death, and they hid his body in the fish crib. Their evil had ended up on her doorstep, and now people in Arbor Vale wondered if her husband or Jim had been responsible for Clive's murder. Shock yielded to fury.

"This is your fault," Beatrice snarled. "You should have emptied Clive's pockets. We dumped his body with the necklace, and that's evidence against us."

"Don't put this on me," Floyd said. "You have two hands. His pockets weren't on my to-do list."

"If only we had noticed the necklace was missing," Beatrice said. "Everything we've built is ruined because that reporter had to nose around the fish crib. Finding that necklace brought her right to our door. Everyone in town had heard the story of Clive selling Suzanne's necklace to us for a hundred dollars."

"The fool terrorized us," Floyd said.

Beatrice gave a derisive snort. "If I hadn't whacked Clive with that crowbar, he would have killed you for sure. Suzanne must have been relieved when Clive disappeared. She probably believed he left with the necklace. That's probably why she never bothered to contact us."

The van hit a rut in the road. Zita bounced, banging her head on a crate. She gritted her teeth to keep from crying out. At the mention of the necklace, her thoughts returned to the day Brandy made that dive by the crib. Kimmy had mentioned that Brandy had acted a little weird afterward. Apparently, she had confronted the Torkels with the necklace as evidence.

"You should have known better than to have any dealings with Clive," Floyd griped. "He was mean and short-tempered. You got greedy, and now we're paying for it."

"Don't even go there. You've enjoyed all the money I've made," Beatrice snapped. "Slow down, we're coming to the river. Let's dispose of our two complications in the back,"

In a panic, Zita looped the rope around her left wrist. She slumped back on the floor, twisting the loose end as best as she could around her right wrist.

The van jerked to a stop. Beatrice and Floyd got out and opened the back doors. Help wouldn't arrive in time, and Zita couldn't fight them off alone. She said a final prayer for Brandy and herself.

※✧　✧※

When the phone in the hotel lobby gave a jarring ring, Kyla jerked in Kimmy's arms. Zinnia rushed to answer it. Immediately she started to wail and babble. "Oh, Jim, yes, Deidre has been found, safe. But something terrible has happened. Zita has been kidnapped by the Torkels. They're going to drown her."

Knowing the impact Zinnia's outburst would have on Jim,

Kimmy stood and carried Kyla to the reception desk. She pried the phone away from Zinnia. "Jim, yes, it's true. Roger and every available officer they could find are out covering all the river crossings. Daniel went out on his own to help." She shifted Kyla higher on her shoulder. "If anyone can survive it will be Auntie Zita. I'll call as soon as I hear anything. Drive home safely please, and pray."

Zinnia wrapped her arms around Kimmy and Kyla. "I'm so frightened," she sobbed. "What if I never see my best friend alive again?"

Tears gathered in Kimmy's eyes. She refused to even consider that possibility. "Zinnia, this waiting is horrible. But we need to be strong. You understand Auntie Zita better than anyone. She's a fighter and smarter than the Torkels."

Zinnia snuffled and pulled away from Kimmy. Her lips twitched into a slight smile. "You're right. The Torkels have met their match."

❋✕ ✕❋

Beatrice and Floyd roughly grabbed Zita. Beatrice had her feet and Floyd hoisted her under her arms. As they tossed Zita off the bridge, she used every ounce of control to remain limp. If they knew she had regained consciousness, her meager thread of hope would vanish.

Zita hit the water hard, holding her breath. The impact and cold water stunned her. Dazed, she tore at the ropes and removed the tape from her mouth. She swam a few strokes to conceal herself under the bridge. She fought to find a foothold along the river bottom, the current tugging viciously at her clothing. If she slipped and fell, the current would carry her under. Finally she regained her balance and waited. Shivering and teeth chattering, she knew she needed to get out of the water quickly. In mid-May the ice had only been off the lakes and rivers a few weeks.

Hypothermia setting in was a real threat to her survival.

Brandy's body hit the water with a splash.

❊❀⟨ ⟩❀❊

Daniel drove as far above the speed limit as he dared. The twists and turns around blind curves were treacherous. If he ended up in a ditch, or worse, he wouldn't be any help to Zita.

Zita. He couldn't lose her. Not now.

As Daniel passed a car, his foot tapped the brake. Time. Time was passing. If the Torkels harmed her in any way… The possibility of Zita drowning in the cold river filled him with rage. His foot pressed down hard on the accelerator.

❊❀⟨ ⟩❀❊

Desperation forced Zita to take the chance that the Torkels might see her. In Brandy's weakened state, she might not regain consciousness and loosen the ropes. Swimming the short distance to where Brandy had sunk beneath the river's murky surface, Zita plunged under. She saw a dark shape near the bottom. With what little strength remained, she kicked hard, fighting the current.

Zita grasped the back of Brandy's shirt and shoved off the river bottom with all her might. She came up, choking and sputtering, pulling Brandy with her. Zita floundered, unable to gather the strength to pull Brandy to shore.

Out of nowhere a hand forcefully cupped Zita's chin. Too weak to fight or fear, she felt herself slipping away.

"Don't give up on me now, woman!"

The words penetrated Zita's numb brain. *Daniel.*

"Hold on to Brandy and kick for all you're worth!" he shouted.

Zita's legs were deadened from the cold. She could barely feel

169

them, much less move them. Gritting her teeth, she used what little strength remained in her legs. Daniel could drown if she didn't help him. Her hand clenching Brandy's collar remained rigid and clamped tight.

When Zita's foot grazed the river bed, she actually believed they might survive. Daniel released his grip on her chin and stood. With both hands under her arms, he dragged her and Brandy onto the river bank.

"Don't move!" he shouted.

Exhausted, and traumatized, Zita found it easy to obey his orders. Daniel pried her fingers from Brandy's collar. They remained bent, with sharp needle-like shooting pains running the length of each finger.

As Daniel lifted Brandy from the water, he staggered. Zita feared he might pitch forward into the current. Regaining his balance, he carried the young woman to shore.

"She's alive. I need to get both of you to a hospital." Shifting Brandy higher across his shoulder, Daniel started climbing the hill back to the road, his breathing ragged. "I'll get her in the truck with a blanket and the heater on. Then I'll come back for you."

Zita managed to stand and take a few shaky steps. She sensed Daniel was at the limit of his strength. At the base of the hill, she started to crawl. "Keep moving," she mumbled.

A few loose stones skittered past her. Daniel's shoes appeared in her range of vision.

"I told you to wait." His voice was rough with anxiety. "Can you stand?" He lifted her to her feet.

Zita legs wobbled like Jell-O and she gripped his arm to keep from collapsing.

Holding her tight, Daniel placed her right arm around his neck. His left arm was wrapped tightly about her waist. Slowly one step at a time, he half-carried and half-dragged her to the road.

After lifting her into the warm truck next to Brandy, Daniel covered Zita with a blanket. Brandy shuddered, coughing and gagging. Zita recognized this as a good sign. The young woman was alive. Zita gave thanks that she, too, was alive and breathing. Daniel had saved them both. She wondered how he had found her and if Deirdre was safe. Those were questions that could wait. For now she concentrated on keeping her teeth from chattering.

As Daniel pulled on a dry jacket, he was pale and shivering. After putting the truck in gear and heading back toward town, he put in a call to Roger. "I have Zita and Brandy with me. Send an ambulance." He gave their location then added, "Fortunately for them, the Torkels got away." A muscle quivered angrily in his jaw.

The Torkels. In the struggle to survive, Zita had forgotten them. She found it hard to believe they had been fencing stolen property. Even now, she had trouble wrapping her brain around the fact that Beatrice had killed Clive Chatwyn. Would that be considered self-defense? The police would have to sort it out later. Trembling, she clutched the blanket higher. Would she ever be warm again?

Brandy hadn't regained consciousness but the coughing had stopped and her breathing steadied. "We're getting too old for this," Zita mumbled.

Daniel nodded. "You're telling me."

Rounding a bend in the road, they met an ambulance and two squad cars.

CHAPTER FIFTEEN

The heated blankets they wrapped around Zita in the hospital eventually stopped her shivering. Her muscles ached from exertion and her entire body was overwhelmed from exhaustion. She pressed both hands over her dry, tired eyes, wondering where she had lost her glasses. As hard as she tried to block out the vivid memory of her ordeal, the policewoman assigned to guard her door made it difficult to keep the fearful memories at bay.

After a thorough examination in the emergency room, the doctor gave permission for her to go home shortly. An aide brought in steaming chicken noodle soup and peppermint herbal tea. Soon Zita warmed from the inside out. But she longed to scrub the smell of the river water off her body. It remained a terrifying reminder of her encounter with death.

Daniel had refused any medical treatment. He had gone home to change into dry clothing. But Zinnia, Kimmy, and Kyla stayed clustered around Zita's bed. They needed constant reassuring that she was fine. But she didn't discuss her nightmarish experience. And for once Zinnia didn't push for details. Zita wanted to report the conversation she had overheard between Beatrice and Floyd to Roger first.

Brandy had been treated in an adjoining room and then removed to stay on another floor of the hospital. She was dehydrated and needed rest. The doctor reassured Zita that the young woman would have a complete recovery.

The only remaining obstacle was apprehending the Torkels. Zita prayed that they would be captured before reaching Canada. The couple would be charged with kidnapping, attempted murder, manslaughter, and fencing stolen property. After the ordeal they had put both Brandy and her through, Zita hoped Beatrice and Floyd would spend the rest of their lives in jail. Arbor Vale would be rid of the obnoxious, troublemaking couple forever.

When Jim and Heather arrived at the emergency room, there was another flurry of activity over Zita's condition. Zinnia jabbered on half hysterically. Zita leaned back against the pillows and sipped her tea. The memory was too fresh. The terror lingered. She wanted desperately to go home and snuggle in her Morris chair. The special chair she had inherited from her aunt Elsie. Maybe then she could put this day behind her.

Heather bent down and kissed Zita's cheek. "We were frantic on the trip home. I'm so thankful you're safe. And Brandy too."

"Thank you, sweetie." Zita could only wonder why these things kept happening to her. She didn't seek them out. They turned up at her door unwanted.

"You can get dressed now, Mrs. Stillman. Your release papers have been signed," a nurse said entering the room. She herded everyone out. "Let's allow her some privacy, please."

On the way out the group debated who would be driving Zita home. The nurse grinned. "Must be nice to be this popular."

The policewoman stepped away from the door to answer a call on her cell phone.

All Zita's uneasiness and fear slithered back, causing a shiver to thread its way down her spine. Her fingers gripped the bed rails. "Brandy and I are safe. I have nothing to fear," she repeated under her breath.

The nurse poked her head in through the curtain. "Do you

need help dressing?"

"Thank you, but I'm sure I can manage," Zita replied.

A few minutes later the nurse wheeled Zita into the reception area. "We flipped a coin and I won," Kimmy announced. "I'll bring the car to the entrance."

"We'll call you in the morning, Mom," Jim said. "Get some rest." He placed an arm around Heather's waist. "I need to get this mother-to-be home for some rest too." He beamed at his wife.

Her son's happiness filled Zita with joy. How thankful she was to have survived today and to be given an opportunity to live to enjoy those grandbabies.

"Do you want me to stay with you tonight?" Zinnia offered. "I'm afraid to leave you and Kimmy alone."

"I'm fine," Zita assured her, motioning toward the policewoman. "I assume she will be accompanying us home. We'll talk tomorrow."

"I plan to go to the funeral for Suzanne Chatwyn. It's at eleven," Zinnia said.

"I'd forgotten. If I feel up to it, I'll join you there," Zita said, troubled by feelings of sorrow and regret for Suzanne and Jodie. They had been living all these years not knowing what had happened to Clive. Possibly fearing that he would return.

It was important for her to give Roger a full report of everything that she had overheard in the van. There were things she had learned that Jodie would need to be told.

The policewoman approached Zita. "I won't be escorting you home," the officer said.

"The Torkels have been caught?" Zita asked. Her voice sounded sharp and jarring in her ears.

"I'm not at liberty to say. But you needn't worry; it's safe for you to return home."

Safe? Zita wondered if she'd ever feel safe again. She wanted her questions answered about the Torkels. But the officer had made it clear that any further information was confidential.

Kimmy parked the car in front of the main entrance. A nurse

returned and wheeled Zita out, helping her into the car. Kyla jabbered happily in the back seat, "Mama zizi."

Zita laughed. "Did she say 'zizi'? I like the sound of Auntie Zizi."

"It sounded like that to me," Kimmy said. "My baby is getting smarter every day."

The two women sat silently on the ride home, listening to Kyla's delightful chatter. More than anything else, it reminded Zita how blessed she was to be alive.

After Kimmy pulled the car into the garage she asked, "What happened to your police escort?"

"She was relieved of that duty," Zita explained. "Unfortunately she wouldn't say why. I can only hope it means the Torkels have been caught. And that neither Brandy nor I am in any further danger."

※✗ ✗※

Zita had taken a hot shower and snuggled in her warmest pajamas and bathrobe. She was now settled comfortably in the Morris chair. As she raised a cup of tea to her lips, the doorbell buzzed. Irritation threaded through her. Who would have the nerve to disturb her tonight?

Kimmy went to answer the door. She returned, leading Roger into the living room.

Roger's grave expression sent a tremor of foreboding through Zita.

"I need to speak with Zita alone," Roger said. "I'm sorry to disturb you tonight but this has to be handled now."

"Are you okay with this, Auntie?" Kimmy asked.

"Yes, I'm fine," Zita answered. She had a list of things to tell Roger privately. Now was the time to explain the things she heard Beatrice and Floyd arguing about in the van.

Roger waited until Kimmy left the room before sitting down

across from Zita and removing a small tape recorder from his pocket. "Let's start at the very beginning when you were searching for Deirdre."

"The Torkels?" Zita asked. "The police guard is gone, and you wouldn't be here if they hadn't been captured. I have a right to know."

Roger's jaw tensed. "After their attempt to drown you and Brandy in the Flambeau River, there was a high-speed chase. Their van missed a turn and they crashed through a guardrail, ending up in the East Fork of the Chippewa River. They're dead."

Dead. Zita's emotions ran the gamut of horror to relief. The nightmare was over. With a shudder, she clasped her hands tightly together. There were many unanswered questions. Questions she wouldn't ask. Had the crash killed them? Or had they drowned? Had their fate played out the way they planned to kill her?

"Zita, are you all right?" he asked softly. "Can I get you a glass of water?"

She stifled hysterical laughter. *Water? How much of that nasty river water had she swallowed today?* The doctor had given her medication to prevent any bacterial infection. "Let's do what we need to do."

For the next half hour, Zita replayed every intense moment for Roger. Occasionally he would stop her and ask a question for clarification.

Zita worried whether Roger would believe that the Torkels were responsible for Clive Chatwyn's death. She hoped he knew her well enough to trust that she wasn't shifting the blame away from her family. The Torkels were dead. They couldn't defend themselves. Was there a way to prove her allegations? Would Brandy be able to back her up? And what had happened to the necklace?

When Zita finished, Roger said, "I'll type up your statement. Will you be able to come to the station tomorrow and sign it?"

"Suzanne Chatwyn's funeral is tomorrow morning. I'll stop

by after the visitation."

"I'm thankful you and Brandy are safe," Roger said. He grinned, adding, "You are one gutsy, resourceful woman."

Heat worked its way up into Zita's cheeks. She quickly changed the subject. "How is Brandy?"

"She's conscious and resting. Not up to talking. She apparently ingested more river water than you did. I'll get her statement in the morning." He stood, preparing to leave. "I received a call from Brandy's editor. She sent him a report of her dive and finding the Chatwyn necklace and her intention of confronting the Torkels with this information."

"The necklace? The necklace has been found?" Zita asked.

"Brandy sent it to her editor. We'll continue our investigation. But for now Beatrice and Floyd are alleged to be responsible for Clive's murder."

A swoosh of relief like air from a balloon left Zita emotionally drained. *Vindicated.*

❋❨   ❩❋

Monday morning when Zita entered the funeral home, the room resonated with the low murmur of respectful voices. That and the overwhelming scent of flowers. The combination of the two brought back the memory of the funerals she had attended during the past year. It left her with an acute sense of loss and regret over so much suffering and death.

Zita shoved the old pair of glasses higher onto the bridge of her nose, wishing again for the pair that had been lost during the kidnapping. People were staring at her and whispering. With a long, exhausted sigh, she stepped farther into the room, keeping her eyes averted. This unwanted attention was embarrassing and annoying.

Zinnia zoomed in, linking arms with Zita. "Did you get enough rest, cousin? You look better."

Better than what, Zita wondered. The strain of fighting the river current left the muscles in her legs and arms sore and tender. Whenever she moved during the night they throbbed, waking her. Then the nightmare of panic would return in a wave of memory.

Leaning in, Zinnia whispered, "Is it true the Torkels are dead? Did they drown?"

"Yes, they're dead. The coroner will have to determine the cause," Zita said, keeping her voice low. She suspected the questions would keep coming.

Disappoint slid across Zinnia face. Apparently Zita's response hadn't fulfilled her gossipy expectations.

Roger entered the room, taking the attention from Zinnia and Zita. When he walked straight for Zita, the murmuring voices raised a level. Embarrassed heat spread from her neck up into her cheeks.

Zinnia gripped her arm and said, "Now maybe we'll get some answers."

Roger's expression was shuttered. Without a word, he reached in his pocket and removed a pair of glasses, handing them to Zita. "These were found in the van. I assume they are yours."

"Thank you," Zita said, accepting them gratefully. She removed the uncomfortable old pair. "I was afraid I'd have to visit my eye doctor and wait a week to have them replaced." Zinnia's grip tightened on her arm.

"How did the Torkels die?" Zinnia demanded in a shrill voice.

Exasperated with her friend, Zita took a step away from her.

Roger's expression darkened at the outburst. Immediately the room grew silent, waiting.

But Zinnia was undeterred. "Did they kill Clive? Is that why they kidnapped Brandy? Is it true the necklace has been recovered? Is there a next of kin?"

Zita took another step back to distance herself from Zinnia. When Roger turned in Zita's direction, she gave a slight shake of her head, hoping he'd realize she hadn't discussed any of this.

As Roger walked away, he replied curtly, "No comment."

Those two words left a mound of unanswered questions behind. Zita hoped the pieces would come together so she could move past this horrifying incident.

"Well, isn't Roger a fount of information," Zinnia huffed. "Have to buzz. One of the girls is helping me with a new hair product I need to experiment with. Catch you later."

When Zinnia left, Zita knew she had only been given a reprieve from gossipy questions. After a brief conversation with Jodie and Kenneth, Roger returned to speak with Zita.

"Don't forget to stop by the station to sign your statement." Without waiting for an answer, he strode out of the funeral home.

An excited buzz filled the room as everyone's attention turned toward Zita. She decided to follow Roger's lead and exit as quickly as possible. Moving through the crowded room, she worked her way to the front. After giving Jodie a brief hug and acknowledging Kenneth, Zita offered her sympathy.

"I'm thankful you and Brandy are safe," Jodie said. She stiffened and added, "Even after all these years, Clive was able to be part of this ongoing maliciousness and misery. I pray his evil influence has finally ended."

Kenneth wrapped an arm around Jodie's shoulders, pulling her closer to his side. "It's over, and your mom is at peace."

Zita saw the tears glisten in his eyes.

"Roger told me that Mom's necklace has been recovered and it will be returned to me when the case against the Torkels is closed," Jodie said. "I understand I have Brandy to thank for finding it. Mom would be pleased that I will have her family heirloom."

A couple walked up next to Zita to pay their respects.

Zita excused herself and scurried toward the exit, colliding with Daniel. His arms enveloped her, steadying her. She hugged him tight, resting her head on his chest. "You saved my life," she murmured into his suit coat.

"Any time," he said.

When she gazed up into his smiling face, her heart step-danced in her chest. Once again, people were staring. Reluctantly, she released him. He continued to grin down at her.

Words stuck in her throat. She couldn't move or speak.

Daniel saved the awkward moment. "Jenna and Deirdre are getting ready to leave. They'd like to say good-bye."

Zita nodded, still staring up at Daniel, his smile mesmerizing her.

"Is it all right if I stop by the house later?" he asked.

"Yes," Zita said, managing only a hoarse whisper.

"Good. We'll talk then." Still smiling, he walked away to offer his condolences to Jodie and Kenneth.

❊⅄ ⅄❊

Zita walked down to the hotel to say good-bye to Deirdre and Jenna. She would miss the brave child who had saved her life.

Jim met her at the door, beaming. "Mom, I'm so thankful the way things have turned out. You and Brandy are safe. And Jenna has great news to share concerning Deirdre." He leaned in, grinning, and whispered, "Crystal and Alistair left. Let's hope they stay away for another ten years."

"That is good news." Zita said, realizing that much of the stress Heather had been experiencing had departed with her parents. "Let's hear Deirdre's good news." She walked into the lobby. Heather and Jenna were standing by the reception desk.

Deirdre bounded up and hugged Zita. "I'm going to live with my Grandma Betty and Grandpa Bill in Appleton. I'll have my own room and everything."

"That's wonderful," Zita said. She ran a hand gently down Deirdre's cheek. "I haven't had a chance to thank you for saving my life and Brandy's. You were very brave."

"Yes, she was," Roger said, entering the hotel. "I'm glad I caught you both before you left. I have something for Deirdre."

He was followed into the lobby by a reporter and photographer from the local newspaper.

Zita walked away to stand by Heather and Jenna. After all she had been through the past few days, she didn't want to be anywhere near people from the newspaper. In fact, she hoped they wouldn't notice her. "What's going on?" she whispered. Both women expressed confusion over the arrival of Roger and the media.

"Deirdre, the town of Arbor Vale would like to present you with this certificate recognizing your bravery in saving the lives of Zita Stillman and Brandy Gardell. And for providing valuable information that aided in apprehending Beatrice and Floyd Torkel," Roger said, handing Deirdre the framed award.

Zita noted his obvious omission of the Torkels' deaths and Clive's murder. Her feelings remained a mixture of anger toward them and sorrow over their possible drowning. She had experienced firsthand that frightening possibility. A verse in Proverbs twenty-eight came to mind that speaks of man intent on evil, falling into his own trap.

The photographer took pictures and a reporter asked questions and took notes. "I'd like a picture with Zita and Deirdre," he said, motioning to Zita.

This was the last thing Zita wanted but she wouldn't make a scene by refusing. Joining Deirdre, she draped an arm across the girl's shoulders. "You and your grandparents are welcome to stay at the hotel any time as my guests."

Deirdre gave an excited hop. "I'd love that. Grandpa would like to go fishing with Uncle Daniel, and so would I."

As if on cue, Daniel entered the hotel. "Are we having a party?"

Zinnia burst into the lobby at full speed. Half her hair had been pulled through a highlight cap and was sticking straight up into the air. She still had the pink beauty shop robe wrapped around her shoulders. Her cheeks were in high color. She wrapped her arms around Zita shouting, "I won! I won!"

The photographer kept snapping pictures of everyone. Zita could envisage Zinnia's reaction when her crazy hairdo made the front page of the newspaper.

Huffing and puffing, Zinnia sounded as though she were hyperventilating.

"Calm down, sweetie," Zita said. "Tell me what's happened. What did you win?"

Zinnia relaxed her stranglehold on Zita's neck. "I told you this contest involved my natural beauty products. And the reality television show. Do you ever listen to me?"

"Of course I listen to you," Zita said, searching her memory for a previous conversation regarding this contest. It filtered back slowly through the haze of all that had happened the past few days. "Tell us everything."

"I'm a finalist," Zinnia bubbled. "The reality show is to be filmed on a cruise ship and the winning original recipes will be offered a contract with a major beauty products company." She shivered with excitement. "The cruise is plus one and you, my dearest friend and cousin, are my plus one."

Zita took a minute to grasp what Zinnia had said. "You're inviting me on a cruise?"

With a twitter of laughter, Zinnia nodded. "We're going to have so much fun."

"I can't leave Arbor Vale," Zita protested. She registered the fact that the photographer continued to snap pictures. Pictures of her. She dreaded the unwanted publicity.

"Mom, this is so exciting. After all that's happened to you, you need a vacation," Jim said.

Much to Zita's chagrin, there was a chorus of people agreeing with him. "When is the cruise and where is it going?"

"We leave the end of August and fly into London. This is a fourteen-day transatlantic crossing," Zinnia explained. "After boarding the ship, we have ports in Cornwall, Ireland, Scotland, Iceland, Greenland, and Newfoundland before arriving in New York."

Excitement stirred in Zita. This would certainly be a dream come true.

"Say yes, Zita," Daniel said.

"Yes," popped out of Zita's mouth.

"Yes, yes, yes!" Zinnia squealed. "This will be the adventure of a lifetime."

"The adventure of a lifetime," Zita repeated. Her dreams of traveling with Lorman had faded with the passing years. An opportunity that may never come again. And besides, fleeing her recent escapades in Arbor Vale for two weeks at sea sounded restful and safe. A whole fourteen days without another murder landing on her doorstep. She smiled at the gathering of friends and family. "Sign me up."

ABOUT THE AUTHOR

Eunice Loecher enjoys living in a small Wisconsin northwoods town, south of Lake Superior. Outside her window stands a thick forest and small spring fed blue lakes. This setting inspired her Arbor Vale mystery series, featuring the two "Z's" Zita Stillman, amateur sleuth, and her sidekick the flamboyant Zinnia Blossom Winwood.

Writing for over twenty years, Eunice was a finalist in the prestigious Wisconsin Regional Writers Award, The Jade Ring. Eunice also had stories included in three editions of the "God Allows U-Turns" series, the Christian version of the Chicken Soup for the Soul books. Then Eunice switched from non-fiction to fiction and began by writing two romantic suspense novels. She now writes cozy mystery as her true calling.

Contact her through Facebook or

euniceloecher@gmail.com

http://arborvalemystery.blogspot.com

Made in the USA
Charleston, SC
30 November 2015